Marriage by Design

ELLEY ARDEN

Author of *Baby by Design*

CRIMSON ROMANCE

F+W Media, inc.

Published by
Crimson Romance
an imprint of F+W Media, Inc.
10151 Carver Road, Suite 200
Blue Ash, OH 45242. U.S.A.
www.crimsonromance.com

ISBN 10: 1-4405-7965-2
ISBN 13: 978-1-4405-7965-3
eISBN 10: 1-4405-7966-0
eISBN 13: 978-1-4405-7966-0

This is a work of fiction. Names, characters, corporations, institutions, organizations, events, or locales in this novel are either the product of the author's imagination or, if real, used fictitiously. The resemblance of any character to actual persons (living or dead) is entirely coincidental.

Cover art © iStockphoto.com/Kupicoo and iStockphoto.com/HowardKlaaste

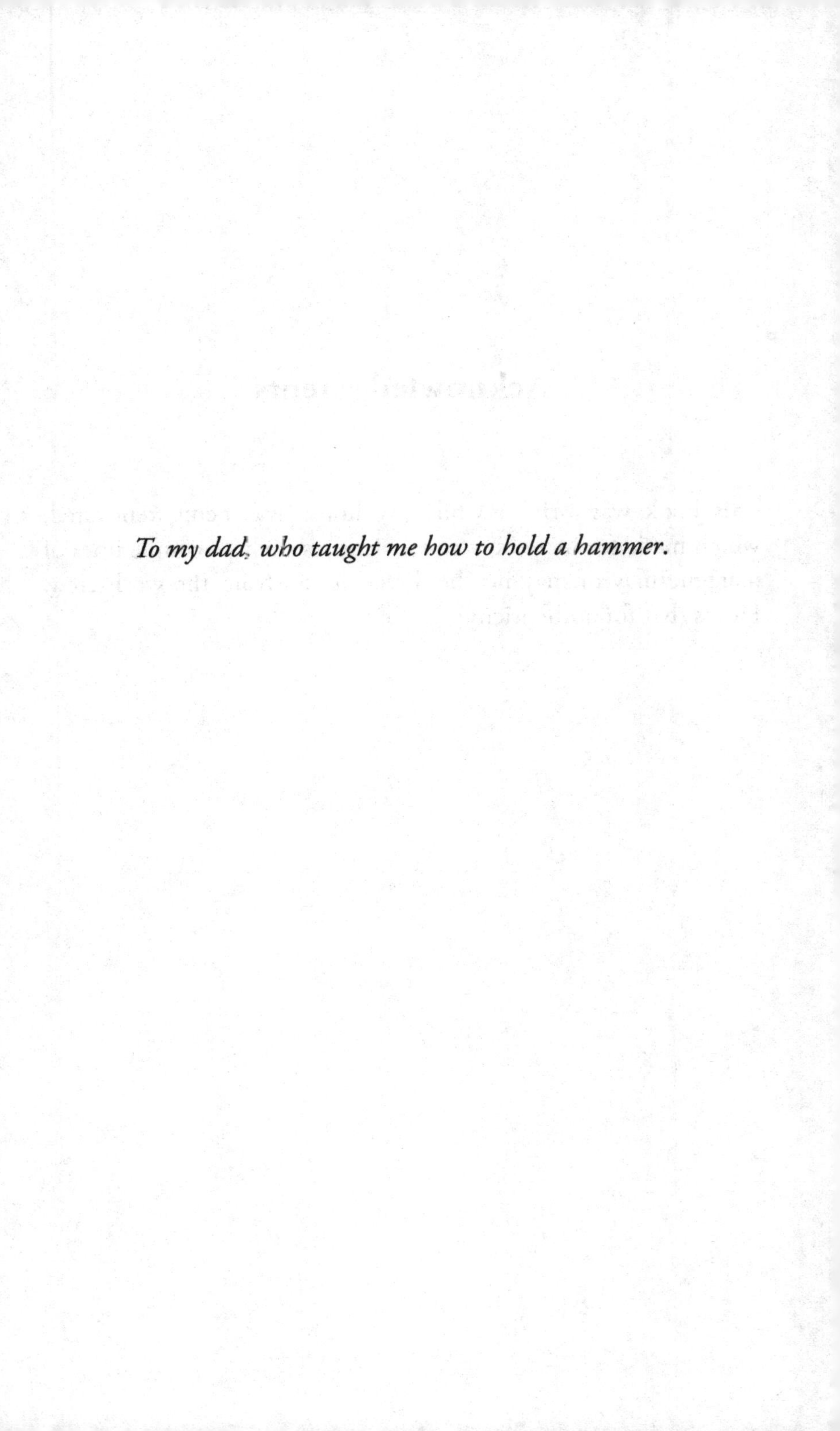

To my dad, who taught me how to hold a hammer.

Acknowledgments

This book was written while my house was being renovated, which made for incredibly convenient research. A couple lines of dialogue may or may not be direct quotes from the work crew. How's that for authenticity?

Chapter One

Oh, hell no!

Angie Corcarelli squinted through the slightly dingy windshield of her pickup against a blast of summer sun shooting off a shed-sized sign. Pounded into the ground outside a line of dilapidated row houses on Pittsburgh's North Side, the billboard read, "Future home of the Parkway Extender. Another project proudly managed by The Perrault Group."

"Oh, hell no!" She whipped her truck around until she was headed downtown again.

Today was supposed to be a good day—a great day—the start of an excellent week. With a cashier's check for seventy-five grand stuffed inside the folder of closing documents on the passenger seat beside her, how could it be any other way?

"Stuart Perrault, I'm going to kill you."

She gunned it through a yellow light and slowed as she dialed her best friend, Trish.

"Trish DeVign Interior Design," answered the perfectly professional voice on the other end.

"That jackass you dated before you married my brother is about to be a dead man."

"Stu? Why? What happened?"

"He's in my way. I've had my eye on some row homes, but the city's been stalling me, saying the properties haven't been removed from the tax rolls yet. Well, guess what? I drove by today, and a big ole sign's up announcing a highway is going to run through the houses, and Stuart Perrault's going to be driving the frickin' bulldozer."

"He doesn't drive a bulldozer. He's simply managing the project."

"Yeah, well, whatever he does," she snorted, "it's gonna be hard to do it *dead!*"

"Ange, you need to calm down. You don't have a legal claim to the properties or even a promise you could purchase them. You got beat out. It happens. There will be other places to flip. Right?"

If only it were that simple. "I want *those* places." Because, if memory served her right, her late father honed his carpentry skills on that woodwork and those rafters. She'd be damned if a highway was going to obliterate any more of his memory.

She swerved into the right lane to avoid backup in the turning lane. A few horns blared.

"Why don't you hang up, and call me back when you aren't driving? I want you alive and by my side when I give birth to your nephew in four months."

Angie backed off the gas pedal with a slight sigh. "There you go playing the baby card again."

"Did it work?"

She wrinkled her nose as she watched the speedometer needle drop to a more respectable speed. "Maybe." Angie adored her three-year-old niece, Angelina, and she couldn't wait to meet her nephew.

"Good. Now promise me Stu lives, because prison would keep you away from the birth, too."

Angie spied the gleaming Perrault Group office complex flanked by fancy landscaping, and scowled. "I'd only go to prison if I got caught."

"Ange … "

"Fine. Stuart lives, but I can't promise he won't be damaged after I get through with him."

Out of the truck, Angie stormed through the parking garage. The cooler temperatures in the shade kept her comfortable despite the work boots, jeans, and stifling anger. How had those properties gone from ripe for rehab in a neighborhood that was supposedly on the rise, to destined for demolition and more traffic than anyone in the surrounding area needed? There hadn't been a single mention of this highway extension on the news or in the paper. Something seemed shady.

She stepped off the elevator into the marble lobby and, for a minute, thought she was in the wrong place. But no, another gleaming sign hanging above a dark walnut reception desk confirmed this was The Perrault Group. What kind of construction engineering firm was decked out like a stuffy bank?

"Can I help you?"

Angie forced a smile at the librarian-like receptionist. "Hi, I'm Angie Corcarelli. I'm here to see Stuart Perrault."

The woman smiled back and picked up the phone. "One moment, please."

Easy. Must've been the boots and jeans. From her appearance it would be clear she was in the construction industry, too.

"Down the hall. Third door on the left."

"Thank you."

He was waiting for her, standing in the hallway outside his office. "Now, this is a surprise."

He didn't look particularly surprised. He looked neutral, like he always did. Businesslike in his navy suit. His cheeks were a little too concaved for her liking, his jaw too square, and the dip in his chin made him seem even more uptight than she already knew he was. The bright blue eyes were nice, though. They just weren't enough to make up for the other things.

"Hey," she said. "We need to talk."

"Is Trish okay?"

"Trish is fine." Not that it was any of his business. Tony, Angie's brother, was the one with a vested interest in Trish now. And, he'd kill Stuart if he knew the guy had even breathed his wife's name.

Now there was an idea.

"Okay." He stuffed his hands in his pockets and tilted his head. "So if you're not here about Trish, then I'm really intrigued."

Again, he didn't look intrigued. Those cheeks stayed just hollow enough to make her notice the shadows on his clean-shaven face, and those pretty-girl eyes never sparked.

She walked right past him and into his office. Construction engineer? She bit back a laugh. It looked like a professor worked here. High-polished shelves were filled to the brim with dustless textbooks, but not a drafting table or blueprint was in sight.

"So what can I do for you?" he asked, rounding his gleaming, pristine desk.

"You can rework the plans for the Parkway Extender to save the row homes you're set to demolish."

He blinked. "And why would I want to do that?"

"Because I was supposed to have first dibs on those properties so I could rehab them."

He nodded, slowly, and then he lifted his hand to his face, pulling on his chin, deepening the dip at the center. She almost laughed at his level of concentration.

"Angie, that's ridiculous. The city owns those properties. They can decide what to do with them. Besides, those houses have been condemned for ages. You can take your pick from hundreds of other urban properties needing rehabbed. I'm not rerouting an entire highway project so you can flip a few houses."

"Fine. Then how about you reroute an entire highway project so the people living there can enjoy their neighborhood? Those houses are a piece of this city's history, and destroying them to put a four-lane highway in the middle of an already struggling area isn't going to make you anyone's hero."

He flinched. *That got him.* She felt a frisson of triumph, but then his shoulders rose and fell, and neutrality returned. "I'm not rerouting the highway. Period. It would unnecessarily and exorbitantly increase costs to my client, and I could kiss my business reputation goodbye. Find another property, Angie. You don't have legs to stand on here."

She hated backing down from a fight even more than she hated giving up on something she wanted. "You know what, Stu?" She wrinkled her nose when she used the silly nickname Trish had always called him by. "I have a hunch you can kiss your business reputation goodbye either way, because I know some people who are going to be very interested in what you're trying to do. The Historic Review Commission will have something to say about homes that old being torn down." It was flimsy. For all she knew they'd already cleared away any red tape that resulted from the buildings' age.

Again, Stuart tugged on his chin, but before he could respond to her veiled threat, there came a knock on his door.

"Come in," he said.

"Stuart, I have … oh, I'm sorry to interrupt. I didn't realize you were in a meeting."

Angie turned her head in time to see an older version of Stuart standing in the doorway. Same chiseled features and bright blue eyes.

"Dad, this is Angie Corcarelli."

"It's a pleasure." The man held out his hand and flashed a blinding smile. He had the personality Stuart seemed to lack. Charisma. And yet, the big grin didn't crinkle an ounce of skin around his eyes.

Not an honest man, her father would've said.

Throughout her fourteen years in the business, she'd met more than a few captains of industry like Alan Perrault. Their steel town roots and rough edges hadn't fully been planed smooth by money and power, and their brash arrogance made them think they could use their charisma to close the gaps.

She straightened her shoulders and reached forward for an obligatory handshake. "It's nice to meet you, too, and you're not interrupting anything. I was just leaving."

He gave her a good, hard squeeze with his hot hand, and then his eyes flashed to the logo above her breast. "Corcarelli Carpentry Company? I've heard that name around town. Residential, right?"

"Yes, sir." She slipped her hand into her front pocket as soon as it was free. Then she turned her head and tossed Stuart a bit of a warning glance. *Don't mess with me, Buddy.* "We'll talk soon."

By the time she made it to her truck, her heart was pumping like a piston. *You don't have legs to stand on here.* She looked down at her steel-toed boots. *We'll see about that, won't we?* As a business owner, she had friends in high places. Maybe not as many as Stuart did, but all she needed was one or two willing to help her with research. There had to be some way to halt the demolition. It was the right thing to do—for the people of that neighborhood … and for her.

She couldn't bear to lose more of her father.

• • •

"What was that about?"

Stuart didn't want to answer. The truth wouldn't make his father happy. "Nothing really." He sat and pulled his keyboard closer. Maybe the illusion of dealing with something pressing would keep his father from asking more.

"Personal or professional?"

"Neither really."

"Jesus Christ, Stuart. Quit giving me the runaround. Why was she here? And you'd better not tell me you're considering using her for a project. She builds kitchen cupboards, not infrastructures."

"I'm not hiring her, Dad. She … well, she's unhappy about the highway extender. She wants us to reroute the project so she can rehab the row houses."

His father's eyes widened. "You told her that was impossible, right?"

"Of course." He wasn't a complete screw up. "I told her a reroute would be exorbitantly expensive and ultimately unnecessary since the city owns the property free and clear."

"Good boy."

Stuart straightened a little at the praise, but then he noticed his father's scowl had returned. "What?"

"She didn't look happy when she left."

"She wasn't."

"Why am I worried that could come back to bite us?"

Because Angie Corcarelli wasn't afraid to speak her mind? And she wasn't afraid to use her big—although, not entirely unattractive—mouth to slam Stuart. She'd done it lots of times when he'd been dating Trish.

"You need to make sure this fire is out. You hear me? I will not have a repeat of Paris."

Paris, where a record-breaking bridge project crashed and burned, because Stuart couldn't change the tide of public opinion once a few opponents revealed that the new bridge would displace a crumbling, inoperable, *historic* one.

Stuart didn't want a repeat of that, either. He couldn't afford one if he wanted to be named his father's successor.

"I understand," Stuart said. "Let me think about it, and I'll come up with a plan."

"No," his father barked. "You said the same thing in Paris. This time, you'll act quickly to make sure it's not a problem. Show some of that Perrault razzle-dazzle I keep hoping you're hiding in there!" He punctuated the command with a showy, jazz hands gesture, then thumped the desk in front of him. "Here's your *plan*. Take a page out of your brother's book and invite her to dinner. Charm her. Give her a reason to think *favorably* about you—if you know what I mean."

He couldn't be serious. Stuart fidgeted. "You want me to neutralize a potential situation by seducing the opposition?"

His father laughed. "Now, now, son. I didn't say that, but … it couldn't hurt. You know what they say: Make love not war." He laughed again, a booming sound that made Stuart flinch.

"You're crazy."

"I'm kidding. But you could still stand to have a little fun with this. Ask her to dinner and smooth out the wrinkles." His father's brows rose. "Or … I'll have Ethan do it."

Checkmate. "Fine. I'll call her."

"Call her now."

He threw up his hands. "She just left the office. She's not going to answer a call."

"Leave her a message."

"Won't that look desperate?"

"Aren't you? After Paris you promised me you'd show more passion and commitment for the success of this business. Now's your chance."

Stuart hid a growl with a clear of his throat and lifted the receiver. With his other hand, he searched for Angie's number in his cell phone. It had to be in here somewhere. He'd texted her a few times when he'd been dating Trish, and he never deleted a contact. Just as he presumed, he found the number (under A instead of C inexplicably) … and she didn't answer.

"Hi, you've reached Angela Corcarelli and Corcarelli Carpentry Company. Leave me a message, and I'll get back to you soon."

He inhaled at the beep and glanced at his father. "Angie, it's Stuart. I didn't like the way we left things. I'd like to take you to dinner, where we can talk more. Call me when you have a chance." Or when hell froze over, because he knew her too well to think she wouldn't see right through this call.

"If she doesn't call back, you call her again," Dad said the second the receiver hit the base. "Be persistent. Don't sit around and weigh the goddamn pros and cons. Sometimes you've just got to act." He walked around the desk and grabbed Stuart by the back of the neck, giving him a playful shake. "One of these days I'm going to get that through your skull. All the shiny degrees and book knowledge in the world can't compete with heart. Passion!" He gesticulated, then waved an open hand, indicating the office. "How do you think I got where I am?"

After his father had gone, Stuart dropped to his desk chair and banged his head against the cushioned headrest. A battle with Angie Corcarelli could ruin any headway he'd made at proving to his father that he was the right son to run this company. Neither his father nor Ethan would let today's little run-in become a major problem. After a few drinks and some laughs, they'd have her eating out of the palms of their hands. Wheeling and dealing always came easy to them.

He straightened. Well, if his father wanted action, then that was what he'd get.

Stuart dialed Simon Cross at City Hall. He'd feel a lot better about everything as soon as he knew the Historic Review Commission had no grounds to oppose the project. Knowing Angie Corcarelli opposed it was bad enough.

She didn't need to be encouraged.

Chapter Two

"He's a weasel." Angie glared at Stuart Perrault's name amid the list of voicemails from yesterday, and then she deleted the message and got back to work. "He just wants to take me to dinner so he can show me some stupid list of pros and cons, which will no doubt prove that I'm a complete idiot for wanting him to move the highway. And then, he'll expect me to beg for his forgiveness. It ain't gonna happen. I don't beg. And unlike you, I'm not impressed by lists."

"Lists can help a person see things clearly. Here, hold this." Trish jabbed the tip of the tape measurer into Angie's belly. "Take it to the woodwork."

Angie dropped the end of the tape to the carpeted floor and held it against the woodwork with her boot. "All I'm saying is, if the guy I dated told me he was going to Paris and had drawn up a cost-benefit analysis to figure out if he should break up with me, I would've told him to stick the pen up his ass."

"Because you're sweet and delicate that way."

"Because I'm honest."

"Ninety-six. Remember that." Trish walked to the other end of the room, dragging the extended tape behind her. "Pull it tight, so we can get the length."

Angie tamped her boot on the end again.

"So, how's this for honest," Trish said. "Stuart is a really decent guy. You're giving him a bad rap. You always have."

She snorted. "If he's so decent, then why did you end up with my brother instead of him? Oh, wait. Because *the list* said so."

"Just because he's decent doesn't mean he was the man for me." Trish yanked on the measurer, sending the metal tape zipping back into its plastic casing.

Angie loved the sound of that. She had since she'd been a kid working side by side with her dad. God, for the last twenty-four hours—ever since she saw that damn sign—she couldn't think about her dad without thinking about those houses being torn down.

Her chest felt hollow. "I think my dad did work on those places."

Trish tapped her fingers over the screen of her fancy tablet PC. "What places?"

"The houses Mr. Decent wants to tear down."

"Ah. So that's why you're so invested." Trish dropped the tablet into her floral bag and rested one hand on her bulging belly. "Why don't you just tell Stuart how much the houses mean to you?"

Angie rolled her eyes. "Yeah. I'll get right on that. Because you know how much I like sharing my feelings with people."

"Then I'll tell him."

"Over my dead body. Besides, I don't even know if I'm right about it. I have no proof my father ever stepped foot on the property."

"Can't you get proof? It seems kind of mean to challenge Stu's project if there's no reason to challenge it."

No, she couldn't get proof. It wasn't like he was the original builder, and that was long before permits were required for simple carpentry work. The houses had been vacant for years and under the management of a revolving door of slumlord owners even longer. She wouldn't even know where to begin tracking down the person who'd hired a small band of Italian carpenters some forty years before. And it wasn't like she could ask her dad or Nonna. They were gone. She still couldn't believe Nonna would be gone almost a full year. And those houses would be gone, too, if she didn't find a way to save them.

Bottom line, even if her father hadn't worked on those houses, someone had. She didn't like the idea of anyone's history being demolished. "A little opposition never hurt anyone. In fact, it makes you up your game. Who's to say there isn't a better option for everyone concerned with that project? Maybe they picked that route because it was easiest or cheapest, not best. Let me tell ya, that neighborhood needs a lot of things, and a highway running though it isn't one of them."

"True. I just wish you weren't facing off against a friend."

"You mean an ex-boyfriend."

"Same thing."

"Only in your world. In mine, ex-boyfriends are the spawn of Satan."

Trish giggled. "Then it's a good thing there aren't very many of them."

Angie stuck out her tongue and went to check on her crew. Damn straight she didn't have a lot of ex-boyfriends lying around. The two who'd meant the most to her had let her down in spectacular fashion. *Ha!* That was an understatement. Both Patrick and Giuseppe could've ended up in jail. What did it say about her that the two times she'd fallen in love, she'd done so with a gambler who bordered on con-artist and a man who'd been twice her age and didn't see a problem with dating an overconfident teenager? Bad judgment. In fact, aside from her father, she was just better off not trusting men. She had enough of them—what with her family-populated work crew—sucking the life out of her already. She didn't need another one.

Although, a man who would suck other things now and then might not be such a bad idea.

When she was satisfied the mudroom cabinets were on track for completion by end of week, she headed off to a charity build for a family who'd lost their home to a fire. On her way there, she called Maddy Gregg at the Historic Review Commission. They'd worked together a couple times since Angie had started flipping inner-city houses. If anyone knew whether or not Angie had legs to stand on, it would be Maddy.

"Give me the addresses, and I'll see what I can find out," Maddy said.

"Wait, so you don't think it's odd that you don't already know what properties I'm talking about? I had to jump through hoops to get permits for the houses one block away."

"If the properties aren't historical, then we wouldn't be concerned with them."

True. But how could they not be historical when almost everything else in that neighborhood was? She didn't get to make that point, because her mother's call beeped through, and she automatically answered. It was habit. For years she'd been answering her mother's calls on the first ring, praying it wasn't bad news about Nonna. Eight months ago, she'd received the worst possible call. You'd think some of the urgency would've passed since Nonna had.

"What's up, Ma?"

"Are you coming to dinner after Nonna's birthday memorial mass on Saturday? Aunt Connie is making reservations."

"I'll be there."

"Good. Four o'clock mass. Don't forget. We can put some flowers on the graves before we head to the restaurant."

It wasn't the happiest way to spend a Saturday evening, but it was important to her family, which was why her crew would be taking Saturday off. The hazards of nepotism.

After the call ended, she made a mental note to gather sawdust from one of her current projects to sprinkle on her father's grave.

She swung her truck into a spot behind a Reimer Electrical Services van and hopped out just as Matt Reimer slammed his door.

"Angie, so glad you could make it."

"I wouldn't miss it." Apparently a lot of people felt the same. Build Together Pittsburgh's first official charity build was off to a banging start—literally. The sounds of hammers pounding and saws buzzing were already at quite a volume, and cars and trucks were stretched up and down both sides of the street. It made her smile knowing there were this many selfless people in the world—people like her dad. He'd have heeded the union's call for volunteers so quickly he'd have been the first one here *and* the last one to leave. Hell, Pasquale Corcarelli could've started a nonprofit like this.

Everywhere she looked, people were carrying boards and tools. They were smiling and laughing. It was exactly where she needed to be if she wanted some perspective.

Up ahead, four guys lifted a wall frame into place. The guy closest to her rocked a sweaty T-shirt, which worked the hell out of a set of admirable biceps. It was odd she even noticed. She worked side by side with physically fit men every day. True, most of them were family, but still … Biceps were biceps, weren't they?

"Looking good, Stuart," Matt called out.

Angie's stomach flipped, and a second later the man with the biceps turned his head enough for her to see his face.

Stuart Perrault. What was he doing here? More important, why was she drooling over his biceps?

• • •

Stuart watched the lethal brunette striding toward him and couldn't decide if it was good or bad luck. She hadn't returned his call, and by the look of her grim face, he figured the thought of a business dinner with him was about as warm and fuzzy as pouring a concrete foundation in January.

Lethal, he thought of the word again, because it was so damn accurate his hair stood on end. That woman in jeans, a T-shirt, and steel-toed boots was dangerous. She could do a lot of damage when she wanted to, like the time she convinced levelheaded Trish DeVign to run off to Cabo for a girls' week, leaving behind a trail of risqué Facebook pictures.

He looked away, because even after four years, he couldn't get one particular picture out of his mind: Angie Corcarelli toned and tanned with long arms shielding her bare breasts from view on a Mexican beach. That picture prompted feelings that sure as hell weren't welcomed when he'd been dating her best friend, and they weren't any more welcomed now.

"Angie," he said, and then he shook Matt's hand. "It's good to see you both."

"It's good to be here," Matt said. He scanned the scene around them. "Is there a check-in table?"

"Inside the white trailer." Stuart pointed to the side yard where thousands of pounds of heavy equipment waited.

"Excellent. Catch ya later." As Matt walked away, Angie took a step to follow.

He should've let her go. He'd said all he'd needed to say in his office yesterday. But his father had asked him to do this, and as a rule, he didn't like to disappoint the man.

"Did you get my message?" Stuart asked.

She stopped and didn't move for the longest time. She was thinking about walking away, wasn't she? He wished she would; maybe then he would stop staring at her denim-wrapped ass.

"I got it." She turned and leveled him with narrowed eyes. "But there was no need for me to respond, because there's no need for dinner."

"I beg to differ."

"Don't beg. It's weak."

He was a lot of things, but weak wasn't one of them. To prove it, he straightened his back and broadened his chest on an inhale. "I don't want to fight with you, Angie."

She sized him up, and an unexpected jolt of awareness charged his body. "Then move the highway."

He was about to tell her she was setting herself up for serious disappointment, when a call for his help from the carpentry tent pulled him away. Thank God. That woman was the last woman on earth he should feel any sort of attraction to—primitive or otherwise. Not only was she the best friend of the woman who was arguably his perfect match, but she was also the sister of a man who hated him. She was brash, outspoken, and intent on causing him more trouble than he deserved. *Move the highway.* He scoffed as he measured and cut two-by-fours.

Still, as the afternoon wore on, every so often he scanned the landscape in search of her. Rule One of any good fight was to keep your enemy in sight. And just as he'd thought, she'd found a sympathetic ear. Verne Moss looked his way, and Stuart had to fight the urge to march over and ask if Angie had turned one of the North Side's biggest developers against him.

When he'd finally finished cutting the boards, Stuart wandered off in the direction he'd last seen her. He wasn't going to beg, but he was absolutely, positively going to get her to agree to dinner. He needed to squash this uprising before it grew to Parisian proportions.

He nearly ran her over as he cut between two dump trucks.

"Oh," she said, stopping just short of him.

"I'm sorry. I didn't see you." He smiled, and her face went a little blank. It made him think he had more of an advantage than he'd thought. "But, I was looking for you." *Pouring on the charm.* His father would be proud. That was really all he wanted. "About dinner."

"Stuart—"

"Angie," he cut her off. "I want to talk about this. You're upset. I don't want you to be upset. We have a lot of history between us.

And despite what happened between Trish and me, I still consider you a friend. I always have."

"Cut the bullshit, Stuart. You saw me talking to Verne Moss, didn't you?" She grinned, and any advantage he thought he had burned away on the spark in her coffee-colored eyes. He liked coffee. A lot. In fact, he should've had a cup the last time he wandered through the refreshment tent. Maybe then he'd have been sharp enough not to walk into a trap like this.

She wasn't any weaker than he was.

"I saw you talking with lots of people." Which was why he was so worried. That mouth could cause him and his project serious trouble.

"Were you stalking me?"

"It's not stalking if you know I'm here."

She huffed. "*Why* are you here? It's a long way from that mausoleum you call an office. Besides, I'm sure there are some overseas conference calls and executive board meetings you're missing while you're over here doing manual labor for poor unfortunate souls you could just cut a check for instead."

"Maybe if you'd spent more time talking to me during the two years I was with Trish rather than bashing me, you'd know there's more to me than my checkbook. I actually like to get my hands dirty."

She didn't look impressed, so he didn't provide any more details. He wasn't sure it would help. The importance of his starting this nonprofit would be lost on anyone but him. Besides, most people took one look at a rich guy with a foundation and saw one thing: tax write-offs.

"Whatever," she said. "Let's just cut to the chase. If I agree to dinner with you, you need to promise me you'll hear me out. I want a fair shot at changing your mind."

"Deal. I'll call you with the details." He could be fair. He was also—usually—unfailingly on target when it came to business.

He'd hear her out. He'd give her a fair shot. But he wouldn't be changing his mind. On the contrary, she'd be the one having a change of heart. It was to be expected. Like he'd said in his office, she didn't have legs to stand on.

But she did have legs. As he watched her walk away, he was reminded of the picture taken in Cabo. Long legs stretched out on a poolside lounger …

Hell, no. He turned around and walked in the other direction, shaking his head. He was not going to entertain those thoughts. For crying out loud, he'd slept with her best friend. He might be desperate to keep this project on track, but he'd never stoop that low.

Dinner. That was it.

• • •

When Angie reached the far side of the lot, she gave a quick glance behind her, fully expecting to find him watching her again. He was a creep—a creep with a nice smile that actually wrinkled the skin around his gorgeous eyes. That little hint of honesty was the only thing keeping her from running him into the ground. Well, that and she would never hear the end of it from Trish.

Huh. Mr. Decent was nowhere to be seen. Maybe he would give her a fair shot after all.

But just in case, she was going to walk into that dinner prepared.

"Hey, did you get those numbers for me?" she called out to Verne who was taking a break on the bed of a pickup truck.

"Yep. You want me to text them?"

"That would be great. Thank you." Having the North Side Neighborhood Society in her corner would help.

She walked on, glancing at the tips of her work boots. Shit. Was she going to have to dress up for this dinner? Stuart Perrault wasn't a pizza-and-beer business dinner kind of guy.

Fine. She would dress up. In fact, if she had to do this, she would shock the hell out of him. Shake things up a bit. She'd wear a dress. Nothing too revealing. Just something that would prove she absolutely, positively had legs to stand on. She saw the way he looked at her from time to time, so she'd use it to her advantage.

Frigging Stuart Perrault with his mind-blanking biceps, movie star smile, and "Ooh, I didn't see you there."

Two could play at this game.

Chapter Three

Stuart exhaled when he passed his father's office and the door was closed. He didn't want to be pulled into a painful end-of-day debriefing. Not on a Friday. Besides, talk about the highway project was bound to lead to talk about Angie. And he wanted tonight's dinner to unfold without added pressure. He already knew what was riding on this.

"Aren't you going the wrong way?"

He looked up to find Ethan at the end of the hallway, blocking his path to freedom.

"Dad called me into his office. Said it was critical. I figured you'd be going too," Ethan said.

A clandestine meeting with the son who hadn't lost control of a multi-million dollar international bridge project? Stuart tugged at the collar of his dress shirt, which suddenly felt two sizes too small.

"I have plans," he said, preferring not to admit he was slighted.

"Gentlemen." Their father stepped into the hallway with a tight-lipped look on his face.

"Well, enjoy your evening," Ethan said, and then because he was a typical little brother, winked and added, "Especially if it involves an attractive dinner date."

Their father perked up at that. "Speaking of dinner dates. Have you wined and dined away our problem, yet?"

So much for avoiding a conversation about Angie. "We're meeting tonight."

"Excellent. I want details," he said, stepping aside so Ethan could pass into the office. "Every single one."

"*Every* one?" Ethan asked, and then he and their father shared an eerily similar, all-too-easy laugh.

Stuart might look like his father, but Ethan's gregarious personality made him the real chip off the old block.

"Okay, maybe not every detail," his father said. "I'll leave the locker room talk to you guys."

"There won't be any locker room talk," Stuart said, looking past his father to Ethan, who was sitting in their father's chair with his feet kicked up on the desk, tossing a rubber stress-relieving ball into the air.

Some days he wished he could be that easygoing. But he couldn't see how sitting back and taking things in stride could help solve his problems. Maybe if he'd been born with a horseshoe up his backside like his brother, but letting things slide always seemed to make things worse for Stuart. Contrary to what his father thought, that was exactly what he'd done in Paris—*ignored* the initial rumbles of the protest. He wouldn't do that again.

The lingering image of Ethan getting comfortable in their father's chair put Stuart in a miserable mood—so miserable he ordered a beer and sat at the bar while he waited for Angie to arrive at the downtown business club. Normally, alcohol wasn't on the menu for a meeting like this. Control was a critical component of success.

But sometime between the first and second glass of Stella Artois, he got lost in the hockey game playing on a television suspended in the far corner. The next thing he knew he was glancing at the door in time to see Angie.

She took his breath away. Her eyes sparkled in the low light, and her full lips shined. The fact that she wasn't smiling should've tempered his enthusiasm, but the alcohol made sure it didn't. He was already following the inky strands of hair down to their tips, where they brushed the swell of her breasts. A white blouse was tucked into a navy skirt that ended a few inches above her knees. And she wore heels. Crazy-high, shiny black heels.

Damn. He blinked, thinking maybe he was seeing things. Two beers was a lot for him. But the men around him appeared to be gawking, too.

"Hey." She slid onto the stool beside him and looked at his empty glass. "Am I late?"

"No. I was early. But, since I got a head start, let me buy you a drink before we head to our table."

"Nope. I'd like to keep my advantage." She smiled a sly, sultry smile, and just like that he was reminded this wasn't a friendly encounter.

He pushed his glass toward the back of the bar and tossed enough money to cover the drinks and tip onto the counter. "All righty, then. Shall we?" He swept a hand toward the hostess's desk.

At a table in the corner of the dimly lit dining room, he lamented his lack of focus while Angie stared at the menu he knew by heart. He should be diving into this discussion with his usual relentlessness. *Back off, or there will be consequences.* But he couldn't imagine saying something like that to her. Why? Because they had history? Or was it because he liked the way she looked? Either reason was ridiculous.

"See something you like?" he asked.

She glanced at him over the menu. "Maybe. You?"

Damn. He bit the inside of his cheek. Those eyes. They were like a neon sign advertising hot, messy sex. Was Angie Corcarelli that kind of woman? She was strong, self-assured. And from what he knew about her, she flipped a middle finger at the rules. Would she follow him to the men's room for a quickie? Slide her bare foot between his legs beneath the table?

Jesus. He choked on his tongue. What was wrong with him?

"The sea bass is good," he said. Healthy. Non-indulgent.

She set the menu down and offered a slight smile. "I'll keep that in mind."

But she ordered the lobster ravioli.

"What's wrong with what I ordered?" she asked when the waitress left. "I saw you wrinkling your nose."

"Too much butter." All that rich cream would tear his stomach apart.

She gave a throaty laugh. "Are you watching calories? God, I can only imagine how many salads you and Trish ate while you were dating. It's a wonder there wasn't a lettuce shortage. Do you order your dressing on the side, too?"

He rolled his eyes. "I'm not watching calories. I'm just careful about things."

"I'd call it obsessive. Neurotic, maybe. Or how about boring?" She laughed again.

He didn't like being made fun of. "Well, I'm glad to see you're enjoying yourself at my expense."

"You don't want me to enjoy myself? Okay then." She steepled her fingers and bounced them off her shiny lips a couple times. "So what would you like me to do? I'm confused. I was expecting hard-nosed negotiating from the minute I sat down, not niceties about the menu. So you tell me how this works. Do we keep acting like it's a friendly dinner until someone says the wrong thing and pounces, or do we go at it over a specific course? I don't know the rules, and I'm sure you, of all people, have rules."

Ooh she grated on him, and yet, those words *go at it* reminded him of that damn Cabo picture. Apparently, his libido didn't seem to care what a pain in the ass she could be.

Focus, Perrault. Or you're going to end up screwing up again. Why did he have those two beers? The alcohol was fogging up his mind.

They were here to talk about the highway project. He'd said he'd be fair. But she wasn't being fair, wearing that skirt and flashing those eyes.

Enough. "How 'bout we jump right in?" he asked. "I want the highway. The city wants the highway. You want the houses. The main problem I see is that you don't own the houses. Considering this highway project is already well underway, I don't foresee any circumstance that would lead to the city choosing one of the alternate routes and selling those houses to you."

"They might, if you revisit the other routes and convince them that relocating the highway would be in everyone's best interest."

She was beautiful, but she was crazy, too. Had she even thought this through? "My client has already spent three years and more money than most people will see in a lifetime on the exploration phase and early engineering. An environmental impact statement, plan preparation, land acquisition, utility relocation ..." he ticked off the completed and nearly-completed tasks on his fingers. "And you want me to ask them to start all over again just so you can flip a few derelict houses? Think about that for a minute."

Her dark eyes turned dead black. "Those houses are more than what you see, and for you to dismiss them as derelict says a lot about your character. Sure, run a highway through them. Who cares? Nobody will miss them." Her voice pitched upward. "Nobody has any memories of sitting on those porches or chopping vegetables at those sinks or hammering nails into those walls."

He would've been more sympathetic had she not ridden her emotions to the point where she was clearly audible to the tables around them. He leaned forward and hissed, "Ultimately, this is not my decision."

"But you could impact the decision! Don't they pay you for your opinion as much as your construction expertise?"

He sat back, exhaling to the ceiling. This was nuts. He was arguing with a woman in public about a property she didn't even own. She was completely irrational and drawing him into it. Her fight was with the city, not him. And yet, he couldn't pass her off without worrying it would come back to bite him.

"Listen." Thankfully, her volume had dropped. "No matter what I've said about you in the past, I have to believe you're a good guy. I mean Trish saw something decent in you. Dig deep, Stuart, and do the right thing."

"You *have to believe* I'm a good guy? Gee, thanks." He scoffed. "No, wait. What did you say about me in the past?" He always had been too damned interested in what people thought about him.

She shrugged. "Nothing terrible. Just that you're cold and unemotional."

Nothing terrible? What would terrible sound like? "Well, I suppose that's to be expected when it comes from an overly emotional person like you."

"I'm not overly emotional."

"I've seen you throw hammers at people."

"You saw that once, and it wasn't even close to hitting the kid. It was a scare tactic."

"Yeah, well, it worked." On him. The kid, who Stuart later learned was her cousin, hadn't seemed fazed. He, on the other hand, had walked away thinking Angie Corcarelli needed to tighten the loose screws in her head before she worried about tightening the ones in the walls.

She grinned. Not the sultry, sexy grin that had him losing his mind a half hour ago, but a sinister one that made his back straighten. "You're scared of me, aren't you?"

"No. I'd simply prefer to not be on the receiving end of one of your hammers."

"Then help me keep those houses intact. Help the people of that neighborhood instead of hurting them with a highway that will cause nothing but noise pollution and exhaust fumes. For crying out loud, most of those people can't even afford a car to use that highway. You're going to be screwing them over so people from Sewickley and Wexford can get to work faster." Her brows rose. "Wait a minute. You're from Sewickley, aren't you?"

"I live in Churchill now."

"I don't care where you live. The point is you're putting the needs of a higher income bracket ahead of the needs of people who have trouble fighting for themselves."

He clenched his teeth. It took a few seconds of staring off into space for the sting of her words to pass. "You don't know me, and you don't know what you're talking about."

"I know enough. You're a man who made a list of pros and cons and then broke up with a woman who'd hung her hopes on you for two long years. And you did it because business came first." Disgust was written all over her face. "Thank God, Trish found my brother. She realized there was more to life out there than what you were selling. You, however, still need to get a clue."

He covered his mouth to hold in a frustrated growl. Trish had been as willing to end the relationship as he had been, but he wasn't going to go into that now. This was supposed to be a business conversation. "You're getting off track, Angie, and you're being unfair."

"Well, you had no intention of dealing with this topic fairly, so now we're even." She smiled at the approaching waitress.

He didn't feel like eating. Angie had him all wrong, and he stewed about it until the waitress left.

"Listen," he said. "I wish to God I could let your poor opinion of me slide, but for some reason I can't. You think I like this …" He snapped his mouth shut on a wave of common sense. Voicing his discontent to a potential adversary about the way things were playing out at work wasn't going to help him.

She set her fork down and leaned forward. "I think you like what?"

He shook his head, wishing he could take back every word. "Never mind."

"Stuart." Paul Frost, a grocery chain magnate, seemed to come out of nowhere. "I apologize for interrupting your meal." He smiled at Angie. "I won't keep you. I wanted to commend you on the recent build and tell you we'd like to donate bottled water and fresh fruit for the crews going forward. It's the least we can do to help you get this nonprofit off the ground."

Stuart hoped the tension of the last few minutes wasn't written all over his face. He forced a smile, as he glanced around the room and wondered if Paul had been sitting close enough to hear any of the heated conversation. What a mess this evening was turning out to be.

"That's incredibly generous," he said, reaching out to shake Paul's hand. "Thank you."

They exchanged a few more sentences about whom Paul should contact to set the ball rolling, and then the man was on his way, leaving Stuart with a quizzical Angie.

"Why was he acting like you have something important to do with Build Together Pittsburgh?"

"I'm the founder."

Her pretty, pointed chin dropped, and her mouth opened.

"Not what you'd expect from a heartless man who puts higher income bracket people ahead of people who struggle to fight for themselves, huh?"

She glanced away from him and then back again, her face suddenly much softer. "I'm sorry." Her noisy exhale gave Stuart even more satisfaction than her apology had. "I didn't know. Maybe I was being a tiny, tiny bit too hard on you."

He smiled. "A tiny bit, huh? I'm not a bad guy, Angie. I'm just in a bad place as far as this highway project is concerned. There's not a lot of wiggle room."

But suddenly he wished there was. He laid his napkin on the table and studied her.

"I'll tell you what. I will look over those plans again for any possible way to keep those houses intact, and if I can't manage that, then maybe you could convince the city to sell you the row homes on the condition that they be moved to a vacant property."

Her brows rose, but a second later she was narrowing her eyes at him again. "And if that doesn't work?"

He shook his head. She drove a hard bargain. "If that doesn't work, then I'll figure out a way to give that neighborhood something even better in return. Park space, neighborhood gardens, business district facelifts. We can get creative. You can help." Her skepticism remained. "Come on. Give me a chance. Just please … promise me you won't go stirring up trouble before I've given this my best shot."

● ● ●

Angie stared at the frustratingly handsome man who sat across the table from her. The stuffed suit who'd dumped her best friend like the woman had been a stop on the corporate ladder was also the guy who'd started Build Together Pittsburgh? She couldn't believe it. He sounded so … reasonable. She could move the homes—*if* she could secure the deeds. It would cost her more than a straight rehab, but if that were the only way to save the houses from demolition, it would be worth it to preserve her father's legacy.

"Fine," she said. "I'll back off. As long as you keep me in the loop. But if I think for a minute you're playing me just to keep me quiet, then I'll fight back even harder."

"I'd like to avoid that." He smiled. "Especially if we're in a room with hammers."

She rolled her eyes, but couldn't keep herself from smiling, too. "I can't believe I didn't know you were behind BTP."

"There are a lot a people behind BTP. I just came up with the idea."

Still, it was impressive. And he wasn't even gloating.

He reached into the breadbasket, the motion showing off an angry bruise on his thumbnail.

"Did you swing and miss?" she asked, lifting her hand and pointing at the injury.

His deep laughter spread warmth across her chest.

"Yes. Yes, I did. I guess I'm a little rusty."

He hadn't looked rusty that morning. Her head filled with memories of his biceps flexing as he helped lift the framing. The warmth spread across her face, and she drained her ice water for relief.

"Too much time in that stuffy office," he said. "I need to get out more."

And yet she'd always thought that stuffy office was exactly where he wanted to be. "So is that why you started BTP? To get out more?"

"No. It started by accident. You remember the Christmas Day house fire on Mt. Washington that killed two kids a couple years ago? That house belonged to my high school hockey coach. I had to do something to help, so I put together a crew to offer low- and no-cost construction when he was ready to rebuild. It was hands down the most rewarding thing I'd ever done, and I wanted to do it again, so Build Together Pittsburgh was born." He beamed with pride, and the unguarded smile—maybe the first of its kind she'd seen from him—took her breath away. "The overwhelming support from the community has been humbling. People are really surprising."

You're telling me. This dinner had been nothing like what she'd expected. No ruthless warning that she needed to back off or risk the wrath of his family's money and powerful contacts. Not a single dig at her brother or question about Trish—even after she'd baited him about them. Tonight, Stuart Perrault had been a respectful, reasonable guy. He was easy on the eyes, too.

But she wasn't stupid. He had flaws. They all had. And he was only reasonable now because she hadn't given him anything to be unreasonable about. She'd backed off willingly.

After dessert, he offered to walk her to her car, but she declined. Things were already too weird between them. She needed space, not an escort. Before she walked away, he promised to call her later in the week to let her know what he'd come up with. She wished that didn't put an extra bounce in her step as she made her way across the street to the parking garage.

What the hell is going on with you?

When her phone rang a few feet from the garage entrance, she figured it was Trish wanting a rundown of the evening's events. *That* turned her stomach inside out.

Instead, it was Maddy Gregg. "Are you still interested in halting this highway project?"

Angie's feet stopped a second before her heart did. "Why?"

"The city is required to give the public opportunity to comment on proposed changes to historic properties. We've found no such opportunity existed—not even a posting on the buildings. I believe that's what's called the smoking gun."

A horn sounded behind her, and she turned to see Stuart driving by, waving and smiling as he went.

He wasn't going to be smiling when he got a load of this.

Chapter Four

"Please tell me he's not lying at the bottom of the Allegheny River with a cinder block tied around his neck or cemented into the basement floor of some house you're rehabbing."

Angie looked up from the cabinet she'd been planing and glared at Trish. "You know, you're one of us now. You need to stop with the fricking mob stereotypes. Stuart is fine. He probably spent the weekend soaking up sun on the golf course. Dinner was fine, too. Completely civilized … mostly. And if I ever decide to off somebody, I'll use my hammer."

"You're lucky I get your warped sense of humor," Trish said. She dropped her frou-frou bag beside the door and walked into the garage. "Those look good." She pointed to the finished cabinets propped against a wall. "Are we on target for installation tomorrow?"

Angie nodded.

"Good, then you'll be done here and can start the hardwood floors over at the Wright house."

Angie nodded again.

"Great. So now that we've got the critical work stuff out of the way, let's revisit the dinner topic. How did you two leave things?"

She didn't want to think about Stuart, let alone talk about him after Maddy's phone call had put her in such a shitty position. She'd spent the weekend at a string of exhausting, never-ending flea markets, digging through bolts of fabric and piles of yarn with her craft-happy mother just to push thoughts of Stuart and the row houses away. But Trish wouldn't accept silence. She'd badger until Angie said something satisfying.

"Stuart said he'd look into moving the highway, and I said I'd back off until I heard from him again."

"Wow. Very mature."

"It was."

"I sense a but."

"No 'but.' I said I'd back off. I'm backing off. I didn't think about those houses or talk about those houses for two whole days. It's no big deal."

"Then why is your jaw clenched?"

She opened her mouth to protest and was greeted by a dull ache just below her ears. She hadn't even known she was clenching.

"Listen, I know you don't like him, but he really is a man of his word. If he says he'll look into things, then that's exactly what he's going to do."

"We'll see." Doubting him wasn't personal. "I don't know how long I can sit back, though. After I told him I'd lay off, I got a phone call from Maddy Gregg, my friend at the Historic Review Commission. Apparently, someone didn't follow the protocol needed to initiate the demolition of those houses."

"Which means?"

"Technically, the project can be stopped."

"Does Stu know?"

She shrugged. "Maybe he's known all along. He could be the one who tried to pull a fast one on the community. I don't trust him like you do."

"Wow. So now what?"

"Maddy is speaking at the monthly North Side Neighborhood Society meeting on Saturday night. She's going to let the people know what's going on. She asked me to go, too, but I can't."

"Right. Saturday is Nonna's birthday memorial mass and dinner."

She nodded. It was like having to choose between honoring her father's memory or her grandmother's memory; it wasn't easy. "They'll have to get this ball rolling without me."

"Poor Stu. I hate to see him blindsided. He takes work very seriously."

"I take my family very seriously. I want those houses, Trish. If there's the slightest chance my father drove a single nail into those boards, I want to save them."

"I know. It's an emotional subject for you, but I don't want to see either one of you get hurt. Maybe you could get your friends to listen to Stu once he comes up with some options that would serve everyone involved."

"Sure, give Stuart a heads up that this information has been discovered, so he can pay someone off to fix it and make it go away. Forget that. This could be my best and only shot at coming out on top."

Angie refused to feel guilty about having an ace up her sleeve. After all, if the tables were turned, she didn't believe for a minute Stuart would ignore *his* best shot for her.

• • •

Simon Cross, the head of the Bureau of Building Inspections, sat across the long boardroom table from Stuart. He didn't look happy. Nobody in the room on the third floor of City Hall did. Stuart only wished that being stuck in a meeting on a sunny Friday afternoon was the reason why.

"That property has been condemned for two years," Simon said. "I can't believe this is even an issue."

"There is a right way and a wrong way to go about demolition," said Jana Wright, the assistant city solicitor. "Apparently, whether it be human error or oversight, we've gone about it the wrong way, and someone has figured that out."

Angie, Stuart thought, his pulse racing. Damn it! He'd made the mistake of believing she would back off and not go behind his back to stir up a firestorm. He wanted to bolt from this meeting and track her down so he could tear into her. But no, he wasn't going to let his emotions get the best of him. He would keep his mouth shut and his hands as clean as possible so they could come up with a solution that wouldn't lead to his father getting involved. As far as anyone in this room was concerned, he had nothing to do with this hiccup.

"What's the big deal?" Simon asked. "All we need is to make notice of the demolition and wait fifteen days for the motion to clear without opposition. Nobody wants to buy those properties. Like you said, they've been condemned for two years."

Angie wanted those properties. He clenched his fist beneath the table but kept his face neutral.

"Don't be so sure about that," Jana said. "The North Side Neighborhood Society is getting support from the Historical Review Commission. They're sending a speaker to their monthly meeting tomorrow night. Investors and anyone else with an interest in revitalizing that neighborhood attend those meetings. They're bound to find a buyer."

"You mean sucker." Simon scoffed. "Have you seen those places? Rat infested and graffiti laden. What sort of idiot would invest in something like that when you could build new on any number of vacant properties in the same neighborhood?"

Again, Stuart thought, *Angie*, and his blood pressure rose. What did she have against him that she refused to afford him a respectable amount of time to come up with a mutually beneficial solution? One week after she'd agreed to back off, and she'd gone ahead and gotten the HRC and neighborhood association involved. This was going to hit the nightly news and morning edition, wasn't it? There could be picketing. Just like Paris.

He swore beneath his breath.

"What do you think, Stuart?" Simon asked. "How much is this delay going to cost us?"

The city? "It's just a guestimate, but I'd say a fifteen-day delay at this point would amount to several thousand dollars."

Which was nothing compared to what he stood to lose.

The minute his feet hit the sidewalk, he dialed Angie. Of course, she didn't answer. Under different circumstances, he'd have weighed the pros and cons of leaving a message, but things were rapidly approaching critical. "I don't appreciate being screwed over," he said, barely clearing the beep. "You need to call me."

He needed to know exactly what she'd done, so he knew exactly what he should do.

If her face was going to be plastered all over as the leader of the opposition, it'd be a hell of a lot harder to pass this off as something having nothing to do with him.

His phone rang. The screen announced his father as caller. It figured.

He wanted to ignore the call, but if he did, Ethan would be his father's next call, and he'd be more than happy to pick up. "Hello."

"How was the meeting?"

Muffled noises not unlike that of a lawn mower engine filled the background. A Friday afternoon tee time. Speaking of Ethan. He was probably there.

His brow furrowed. "The meeting was interesting. Everything's moving along on our end, but the city dropped the ball on some permits and now has some additional red tape to work through. We should be able to stay on the original timeline, though." He dropped the receiver so his father didn't hear his throat click when he swallowed.

"As long as the ball dropping wasn't on our end. Now, how about you head over to the club and join your brother and me for the back nine and a few drinks."

Not today. He had some damage control to do.

• • •

Angie popped the top off a bottle of beer and plugged her phone into the speaker system. Classic rock, light beer, and her latest model house creation. Another banging Friday night.

Last week at this time, she'd been dressed up and out to dinner. For the first time in ages. With Stuart.

Well, no chance of a repeat performance there. His brief message had made it loud and clear that he'd found out about the neighborhood society's meeting.

Her stomach hollowed out. *Oh, please.* Why should she feel bad about this? She hadn't called the meeting. She wasn't even attending the meeting. The people of that neighborhood could and should do whatever they needed to do to protect themselves and their homes. Right? Right.

So … if she hadn't done anything wrong, then why wasn't she calling him back to defend herself?

Forget about it. She plugged in her glue gun and lined up a row of extra glue sticks, then she checked the junction points of the Popsicle sticks she'd glued together last Saturday night. The second floor should be framed by the end of the night.

She took another swig of beer. Was it pathetic for a thirty-two-year-old woman to spend her weekends building houses out of Popsicle sticks? She flipped herself off in the dining room mirror before she headed into the kitchen for some pretzels.

She wasn't pathetic. She was comfortable. Satisfied. She enjoyed quiet nights—and fat-ass pretzels. She plopped a broken piece into her mouth and smiled as she chewed. Unlike last Friday, tonight she wouldn't have to put any effort into the evening, except when it came to the model house.

Her smile faded. She was staring at a lifetime of Friday nights like this, wasn't she?

Fifteen minutes later, with the help of some Eagles music blasting from the speaker and one polished-off bottle of beer, she felt better. The guest bedroom and bath had been framed out over the garage, and she'd only burnt her fingers on the tip of the glue gun twice.

When the end of "Hotel California" came, and the song faded, she heard knocking on her front door.

The cable box read *8:30*. Maybe her mother's Bunco game had ended early.

She wouldn't mind a little company.

Stuart stood on her front porch. His face was wrinkled like his dress clothes. "I've spent the last six hours weighing the pros and cons of showing up here, and I just can't take it anymore. I have to know if you're leading this rebellion."

She laughed.

His eyes narrowed.

"Oh. God." She covered her mouth for a second. "You were serious. It was just so funny the way you said it."

"I'm dead serious about anything having to do with my career. Please, can we talk about this? The more I know, the more I can prepare for the fallout."

Intense, but not scary. His cheek pulsed, highlighting the strong line of his jaw, and his messy hair begged for fingers to tame it. Sexy was more appropriate.

She shouldn't let him in, not when she was thinking and feeling like this, but she did.

"First of all, what did you hear?" She stood beside her sofa, but refused to sit. *Don't get comfortable.*

"I got called into a meeting this afternoon, and that's where I learned the Historic Review Commission is speaking at the neighborhood society's meeting, and the focus is on those row homes. I take it you assembled the troops."

She bit into her bottom lip rather than laugh at him again. "I didn't set up that meeting. I'm not even going to that meeting."

"So it's a complete coincidence that you show interest in those properties, and now these organizations show interest too?"

Maybe. She had bent Verne Moss's ear about the situation at the charity build, and she had called Maddy Gregg and asked her to dig around. So, probably not a complete coincidence. "You told me to back off, and I backed off. Anything that's happening now is happening without my encouragement."

"But with your blessing."

"Sure, if it gets me those houses. I'm not going to slap a gift horse in the mouth, Stuart."

"Just me."

She arched an eyebrow. "If you deserve to be slapped, then yes."

He shook his head. "Why couldn't you be easy to push around?"

She chuckled. "What fun would that be?"

One corner of his lips lifted, and some of the wrinkles on his face smoothed out. "What in the world are you listening to?" He looked toward the speaker system on a shelf across the room.

She looked, too. "Uh, this is 'Ventura Highway' by America."

"How old are you?"

"Obviously old enough to appreciate good music."

He grinned, and the last bit of tension fell from his face, leaving a devastating sparkle in his blue eyes. She stepped back instinctually.

Her skin buzzed as his gaze raked her from head to toe. "I take it you're in for the night."

She glanced at her tank top, sweatpants, and bare toes. "Yep. My Friday night consists of music, beer, and ..." TMI. He didn't need to know. He didn't want to know.

"And what?" He looked around the room.

"Nothing important."

"Whoa. What is that?" He walked by her and into the dining room, where the Popsicle stick house waited. "Are you building this?"

"Yep."

"Damn." He bent over and looked in the first floor windows, and then he straightened and looked at her. "Is this for a client?"

She shook her head. "It's just a hobby. My dad and I used to build them together when I was little. I still work on them from time to time." Like every weekend. *Dork.*

He was leaning over the house again, running his fingers along the joists of the second floor. "That's crazy. So accurate. It's structurally sound."

She nodded. It was structurally sound because she was a construction geek.

"You should wire it."

"I've thought about it, but it's an extra step, and really, why do I need the rooms to light up?"

"Because it would be cool."

Huh. Now, there was a word she'd never associated with this hobby. *Cool.* She smiled. Of course he'd think that. Stuart Perrault was a construction geek, too.

"I'd offer to let you to stay and help me out, but I'm sure you have a hot date."

His lips twitched. "Last Friday night was the only hot date I've had this month."

Last Friday night he was with her …

"I'll stay … if you were serious. I'd like to see you work."

This was odd. She hadn't actually expected him to stay, despite the offer. Well, she couldn't renege now. "Okay. Sit, but don't touch anything. I'm going to grab another beer. You want one?"

"Sure."

So, Friday night had become classic rock, light beer, and working on the model house … with Stuart? She put her head in the fridge and opened her mouth for a deep breath. Weird.

The good thing was he didn't seem to be pissed anymore.

When she returned to the dining room, he was pulling clean sticks from the box and stacking them up to form the foundation of what looked like a log-style house.

"Couldn't stand not touching anything, could you?" She handed him a beer.

"It sucked me in."

She watched him drink his beer and then put another layer on his stick structure. "You can glue it if you want."

"Nah, I'm just playing." He looked up and smiled. "Waiting for you."

Again, this was weird. She'd never worked with an audience before. Well, besides her father. She sat, and before long, Stuart being there didn't matter anymore. The sticks commanded her attention. One wrong move, one heavy hand, and she could undo months of progress.

"Did you always want to be a carpenter?" he asked.

She glanced at him as she held the stick wall frame in place, waiting for the hot glue to cool and dry. "I wanted to spend time with my dad, and I liked building things, so when he asked if I wanted to make a few bucks over summer break by working for him, I said yes. All my friends were stuck inside the mall working for minimum wage, and I was making double working alongside my dad. It seemed like the greatest gig in the world."

"You never thought about doing something else?"

"I majored in international business at Duquesne."

"Really?"

She nodded and let the wall frame stand free. "Don't ask me what I was going to do with that. It just seemed interesting at the time. But then my dad got sick, and I backed down to part-time classes so I could work more and he could worry less. And then when I graduated, I became his foreman. And, when he … died … I became the sole proprietor of Corcarelli Carpentry Company."

She smiled. "I was twenty-six and in charge of a crew of ten men twice my age. Good times."

He chuckled. "No wonder you're not easy to push around."

"How about you? Did you always want to be an engineer?"

He tapped a stick on the table, and reached for his beer. "Nope. I wanted to run my father's company, wear the shiny suits, drive the flashy cars, golf every Friday afternoon, and tell my wife I was going to be late for dinner every night. It just so happened the company was an engineering firm, so I figured I better become an engineer if I wanted to be in charge of it one day. Lucky for me, like you, I enjoy building things. Actually, I enjoy the building a lot more than the other crap."

"Like crushing the rebellion?" She winked at him.

His expression changed. He looked more serious, but not angry. His head tilted, and his flawless lips parted while he studied her through bright, blue eyes. He was incredibly nice looking. Gorgeous, really. How was she just coming to appreciate this now? She'd known him for years. *Trish.* That had to be it. She'd never allowed herself to look too long at someone who'd been sleeping with her best friend.

She didn't realize her arms were covered in goose pimples until he pushed his chair away from the table and stood.

"You know what?" he asked. "I should go. I can't believe I barged into your evening like this. My apologies." He nodded his head and walked away.

Okay. She scrambled after him. "I didn't mean anything by the rebellion crack."

"I know." He turned to face her when he reached the door. Again, he looked funny. Like he didn't know what to say, or the beer had upset his stomach. "Thanks for the drink and conversation."

"Anytime." The word caught in her throat.

The lump it made lingered long after he'd gone.

What the hell?

• • •

Stuart sat in his car staring at Angie's narrow house. He'd come here to corner her about the neighborhood society's meeting and use what she knew to his advantage. Instead, he'd ended up wondering what it'd be like to kiss her, to slip the strap of her tank top off her shapely shoulder and run his tongue along the curve to the dip of her neck.

He was thinking with his dick. And a dick couldn't run a multimillion-dollar company.

No more. As far as Angela Corcarelli was concerned, he was done taking his father's advice. If the old man wanted someone to wine her and dine her and figure out a way to keep her quiet, he'd have to find someone else. As much as it hurt him to think of it, even Ethan would do. Because while Stuart had lots of ideas about how to keep Angie quiet, none of them were appropriate where business was concerned.

Chapter Five

Nothing washed away the sadness of a memorial mass, a trip to the cemetery, and a solemn family dinner like a bottle of Sangiovese.

"Should I open another one?" Angie asked, looking around her coffee table at the empty wine glasses.

Heads shook.

Aunt Connie said it was too late, and her son, Vin, had already warned her not to drink too much before he left.

Ma held a hand over her glass. "I have to drive Connie home."

"You should've ridden with us." Tony flung his arm across the back of Trish's chair and patted her shoulder.

"You ladies could always crash here," Angie said. "I have two extra bedrooms."

She opened the other bottle while her mother listed all the reasons why she couldn't get blitzed and spend the night. Church obligations trumped self-pity, and as the Eucharistic minister for nine o'clock mass, her mother couldn't be hung over.

But Angie could.

She poured herself a glass and took a hearty swig. The service for Nonna counted as Sunday mass for her, and she wasn't above drinking alone. If everyone declined another glass, she could polish off the bottle.

"Ange, turn on the game," Tony said. "It should be in the last couple innings."

Sure thing. Anything to take the focus off death. She grabbed the remote off the end table and scrolled through the channel guide while the eleven o'clock news flickered in the background. An image of the row homes on Hazlett Street caught her eye. "What the …" She turned up the volume.

Clarice Martin of the North Side Neighborhood Society says the next step could be legal action to halt the project. Calls to City Hall were not returned.

"Holy shit." It had made the news. Boy, they hadn't been kidding when they'd said they were having a meeting tonight to take action.

"Are those the houses you want?" Trish asked.

Angie nodded.

"What houses?" Tony asked.

"Just some houses I want to rehab." She stared aimlessly at the flickering screen until her vision blurred.

"Looks like you may get your wish," Trish said.

Yeah. So why did she feel squirmy about it? "I wonder if Stuart saw this."

"What the hell does he have to do with it?"

Angie snapped her attention to her brother who was now perched on the edge of the couch, shifting his eyes back and forth between her and Trish. Bad blood ran between the men since Stuart came back from Paris looking to rekindle things with Trish, only to find Tony in her life.

"Stuart is the project manager for the highway construction that hinges on the demolition of those houses."

"How are you going to rehab houses they're going to tear …" Ma's eyes widened. "Angela, do you have something to do with the legal steps that woman mentioned? Are you fighting City Hall?"

"No. Not me personally. I mean, I've voiced my concern about the project, but whatever legal steps are being taken, it's not me. I'm not leading some rebellion." She winced.

"I hope you do," Tony said. "I hope you bury that smug douche and teach him some boundaries. Somebody needs to."

"Babe, be nice." Trish smoothed a hand over his thigh.

Angie tossed the remote to Tony. "Put on the game." She needed to message Maddy and get the lowdown on what happened at that meeting.

Her phone was tucked in the front pocket of her purse, where it had been since before mass started. The screen lit up with two missed calls and a text message … from Stuart.

He probably blamed her.

She clicked through to his message.

Your friends are out for blood. I sure as hell wish I had known that.

She hadn't known that, either. But even if she had, who could blame her for keeping that information from the enemy? She had to look out for herself. Nobody else would. And she hadn't been the one to escalate this. Whatever happened tonight wasn't her fault. If the city—or The Perrault Group—had done their job and followed proper protocol in the first place, Stuart would still have the upper hand. *Yeah.* She'd call him and tell him that.

Tony cheered in the other room.

There was no way in hell she'd call Stuart while Tony was here.

Twenty minutes later the game had ended, and her house had cleared out, all except her brother and Trish.

"I think we've milked all the child-free time we can out of this evening," Tony said. "Ready, babe?" He helped a tired Trish off the couch and tucked her under his arm.

"At least the sitter can walk home," Trish said, flashing a smile at Angie. "That's the nice thing about having four teenagers living right next door."

"Almost makes up for the way those teenagers trample my grass," Tony grumbled.

Angie laughed. Her brother cared about his grass? She never saw that one coming. Then again, she never could have predicted her brother and best friend falling in love in the first place. Talk about a surprise. She'd had her doubts, but in the end, Tony and

Trish worked. They balanced each other out. Trish was much less neurotic, and Tony was much more responsible. Heck, she hadn't seen him really lose his temper in years.

Tony held the door open for his wife, and they both stepped out onto the porch.

"It was a nice evening," Trish said, but as she turned to face Angie, her forehead wrinkled. "Maybe I shouldn't say that considering the occasion."

"Nah. It was nice. It was." She hugged Trish and then Tony. "Thanks for coming back for drinks. It's better than going home alone after something like that."

"You need to find somebody," Trish said.

Angie scowled. "I did not say that so you could lecture me on my relationship status."

"I know, but …"

"No, 'buts,'" Tony said, helping his wife down the stairs. "You heard the woman. Trust me. I sleep better knowing no loser's sniffing around here. We'll see you at Ma's for dinner tomorrow."

"Yep." She was about to go back into the house when Tony let loose a strangled growl and then took a couple leaping steps toward a car parked on the opposite side of the street.

"What the fuck are you doing here?" His voice echoed in the quiet neighborhood.

"Tony," Trish yelled, and dashed across the street after him.

In the low street light, Angie couldn't see who was in the vehicle, but she could see the make of the car. Stuart drove a black BMW … just like that.

"Get out of the fucking car," Tony yelled while Trish tried to push him back towards their car.

Angie hit the front steps in a sprint. "Stop it. Jesus Christ, Tony. Somebody's going to call the cops." Houses were right on top of each other in her Bloomfield neighborhood. A lot of elderly people lived around here, and they spooked easily.

Tony turned on her, wearing an intimidating glare, just as Stuart got out of his car.

"He's here to see me." She darted between the men. "About *those houses*, Tony. It's no big deal."

She heard Stuart scoff behind her.

"You guys, please," Trish said. "Tony, I'm tired. Can we just go home?"

He shot a *drop dead* look at the last man to sleep with his wife and said, "Fine. Ange, you call me if you need anything."

"Tony, I'll be fine." She watched them walk away with her heart pounding in her ears.

"They really shouldn't let him roam free."

She spun on Stuart. "Don't insult my brother. You're the one who came over here late at night and sat in your car like a stalker."

"Because you wouldn't return my calls."

"I was in church and at the cemetery and then at dinner with my family. I just got your text message a half hour ago."

"How was I supposed to know that?"

"You weren't." She threw up her hands. "You're not my keeper. And for God's sake, Stuart, your text didn't say anything about me calling you. You're deranged."

He rammed fingers through his hair and looked at the stars. "Maybe I am. I can't believe you went behind my back and spearheaded a revolt like this."

"Give me a fricking break. I wasn't behind that news story any more than I was behind that meeting."

He looked at her, his gaze narrow. "I don't believe you. I've been thinking about this, and I saw you talking to Verne. I know you have connections on the Historic Review Commission. You're not telling me the whole truth."

"All I did was start some people digging around. I didn't know anything about someone not following protocol until Maddy Gregg called me, and even then, I didn't do anything about it.

Like I told you last night, I backed off the minute you asked me to."

"And it's going to stay that way."

Angie jammed her fists to her hips. "Excuse me?"

"For this project to stay on course, we need to post notice of the intent to demolish for fifteen uncontested days. After that, everything moves forward, and I'm no worse for the wear. So for fifteen days, you are going to keep your goddamned mouth shut."

Her eyes widened until they burned. "Is that so?"

"Yes, because if my father finds out you're involved with this, he's going to …" He growled. "You just need to stay out of this. Please."

If she weren't so pissed at the heavy-handed way he was treating her, she'd be enjoying his little self-implosion. Stuffed-shirt Stuart Perrault was losing control, which meant she was winning.

"I want those houses," she said.

"While the project is stalled, I can get Simon Cross to convince the city to sell the row homes to a qualified buyer who would relocate them. You being the qualified buyer of course. There's no need for legal action or a public battle. We can do this calmly and quietly, and everyone can win in the end."

"Do you even know how much it would cost to move those houses? I'm one person, Stuart. I have limited funds. The city is spending hundreds of millions of dollars on this project, and you think it's better for me to go into debt to move those houses rather than for them to spend a little more to move their highway, even though they didn't follow protocol. It doesn't make sense."

"It does to me."

"Why? Explain to me why they should be rewarded for pulling one over on the neighborhood they're planning to exploit."

A muscle in his jaw twitched. "You are out of line. Nobody is purposefully pulling anything over anyone else. Nobody is trying to exploit anyone. And my allegiance is to my client. I need to do what's best for them."

"Bullshit. You may have a shred of decency in you, but right now I'm seeing an awful lot of arrogance, too. I don't for a minute think this is all about your *client*. You have something to prove, don't you?"

Again he growled, but this time he kept his intense gaze on her. "I can't afford to lose control of this project, Angie."

"And I can't afford to lose those houses."

"So we're at a standstill."

She nodded, her eyes locked on his. Suddenly, heat rushed through her and the hairs on the back of her neck stood.

"You make me so angry," he said through gritted teeth. The skin pulsed beneath both of his ears.

"Too bad," she said, but her voice was low and had lost its bite. "I have to do what I have to do. So, you do what *you* have to. I'm a big girl, Stuart. I can handle whatever you've got."

She felt sure of it … until his head dropped forward an inch and his palm smoothed against her cheek.

What? Her stomach flipped, and her lips parted for air or words, but both got trapped by his mouth fusing against hers.

White-hot heat flooded her body.

Why? But then the tip of his tongue traced her bottom lip, and a jolt of pleasure answered, "Who the hell cares?"

She opened her mouth and kissed him back like the sex-starved woman she was, curling her fingers into his collar, riding a wave of pleasure that puddled between her legs. *This* felt so much better than being angry. Make-up sex came to mind. She always did like a good orgasmic apology.

He wrapped his arms around her and held her against him, where she soaked in the warmth from his body, breathed in the spice of his cologne, and reveled in the swell of his erection.

Mm. It'd been too long since she'd felt like this. A few years. She wanted to grind her hips against him, toss her head back, and ... laugh, because who knew Stuart Perrault was so hot under the dress shirt collar?

Trish did.

Shit. She shouldn't be doing this with him. Angie broke the kiss and stepped back.

Stuart looked confused.

"What was that?" she asked.

"I don't know." He smoothed a hand across his mouth and widened his eyes. "Impulse I guess. I got carried away. I'm sorry." He opened the car door and jumped inside.

Stunned silent, she watched until his taillights disappeared around the bend. "What was that?" she yelled into the silence.

Impulse. She scoffed. No way. He was sneaky. For all she knew that kiss was part of his plan to her throw her off balance.

She raced toward her house, tripping on her front steps. *Ha!* Mission accomplished.

A growl ripped from her throat. Stuart Perrault may have won this battle, but she was going to win the whole damn war.

• • •

Stuart shut his car door and stared up at his parents' sprawling colonial on a deceivingly sunny Sunday morning. He probably should've paid them a visit late last night rather than the detour he'd taken to Angie's house. That would've saved him the irate phone call from his father at 1:00 a.m. ... among other things.

He closed his eyes for a second and inhaled, fully expecting to smell her soft lavender scent. He'd lost control and kissed her. Of all the stupid things to do.

At the top of the driveway, the garage door clanged, and Ethan ducked below the rising slats of wood. "Be warned. He's in no mood. Right now he's on the phone with the mayor."

So his father was taking over the highway project?

Ethan chuckled as he took a few steps back into the garage and lifted a nine iron out of their dad's golf bag, which was propped against the wall. "Don't worry. He's not firing you or anything. He just wants the inside scoop from City Hall. If heads should roll anywhere, it's there."

Stuart shook his head as he headed up the driveway toward the house. "I couldn't sleep last night. I kept thinking about Paris." And kissing Angie, but that wasn't something he'd admit, not when she could pop up as the face of the opposition at any minute. Would his father fire him then?

"Not the same," Ethan said, taking a check swing. "That historic bridge ran through a vibrant section of Paris and had enough foot traffic to warrant serious protest. These houses? They're eyesores. When it comes down to it, who is going to want to save those except a handful of dorky history buffs who are too poor to actually do anything about it?"

"I hope you're right," Stuart said, but again he thought of Angie, who was neither dorky nor poor enough to rule out of the equation.

"One question though, between you and me: Did you not think to check that proper protocol had been followed?"

His jaw clenched. "When the chief of building inspection checks off on a project, it's assumed protocol has been followed."

"You know what they say about the word assume, don't you?"

"Fuck off, Ethan."

"Whoa. Bro, I'm kidding."

Maybe he was, maybe he wasn't. Ethan and his father shared the same warped sense of humor and calculating business acumen. It always put Stuart, the odd man out, on edge.

"I'm just surprised is all," Ethan continued. "Assumptions aren't usually your M.O." He dropped the golf club into the bag and smiled.

Stuart couldn't return the expression. He walked past his brother and into the garage to enter his parents' house, knowing things were bound to get worse before they got better. But they would get better. Things hadn't completely imploded, and even if they did, there were options. He listed them over and over again in his head as he traipsed down the mudroom hall with Ethan on his heels.

His mother brushed a requisite kiss on his cheek once he was inside the breakfast room, and ushered him to his usual seat on the other side of the table. His father, on the other hand, didn't look up from the Sunday paper.

The silent treatment. Nice. Stuart sat and dropped a napkin onto his lap. When he glanced around the table, the front page of the paper caught his eye. The large photo of the houses took up a bottom quarter of the page. *Parkway Extender Project Delayed* was the headline.

He knew the article was coming, because he'd been contacted for a statement. Still, seeing it packed a wallop.

But delayed didn't mean cancelled, which was exactly what he'd told the reporter.

"Eggs?" his mother asked as she reached toward him with a bowl.

He took the offering on autopilot, but kept his focus on his father. "Dad, I heard you talked to the mayor. How'd that go?"

The paper rustled as his father's eyes came into view. "Fine. Fifteen days and then we're back in business."

"What's fifteen days in a five-year project?" Ethan asked.

Wasted money was the answer, because every day they were off schedule cost somebody.

"As long as no one contests," his father added with a bite in his voice. "And that woman will contest, won't she Stuart?"

His back straightened. "No, she won't."

His father glared. "Are you sure about that? Because you have to be absolutely sure. If she contests, we're in a world of trouble."

"Coffee?" his mother said.

"Yes, please," Ethan said, and then his father raised a single finger to let his wife know he'd take some, too.

"No, thank you," Stuart said, grabbing his full water glass instead. "Listen, Dad. I did as you asked. I took Angie to dinner. I talked to her. She was receptive. She was sincere. Technically, this delay has nothing to do with her."

"Until she steps forward as a viable, potential buyer for historic properties that those bleeding hearts would rather see rehabbed than torn down. Then what?"

His mother shuffled around the table, humming an unrecognizable song, like the men in her life were talking about nothing more pressing than the beautiful weather. Her ability to tune them out made him envious. If only he could be so calm.

"I have an idea," Ethan said.

Their father raised a hand. "I'm sure you do, but this is Stuart's problem to fix. What's it going to be, son? How do you propose we fix it?"

The silence played with his head, making the grandfather clock at the end of the room sound like a ticking time bomb. Finally, he exhaled. "We could reroute the highway. The city will have no choice if they want to move forward with this project."

"The taxpayers ought to love that," Ethan said. "And just in time for the mayor's reelection bid. It's a PR nightmare for everyone involved."

"Which is why I just guaranteed the mayor that the project would go off as planned. Stuart, you need to do better than that. You have no choice but to decisively silence your little friend.'

It was like he'd stepped into a low-budget mafia movie, because nothing short of a *Godfather*-esque ending was going to silence Angie.

Again, he reminded himself there were other options.

He squared his shoulders and lifted his chin. "What if I convinced her to secure the properties and then have them moved to a vacant lot in the near vicinity? I mean if she's going after the properties no matter what, then why don't we spin it? Instead of it looking like a fight, it looks like a charitable compromise."

His father's brows rose. "Interesting. Very interesting. That could work—if she has the cash to undertake the move. Talk about turning the tables on this thing. The positive publicity for us would be off the charts. We'd be appeasing those fascist bastards at the historical society and giving the city exactly what we said we'd deliver. That could definitely work."

Score one for him. Stuart suppressed a smile.

"And if she doesn't have the money?" Ethan asked. "I mean, she's going to need a small fortune to rehab those places according to historical restoration law. What if she can't afford to move them and renovate them? Why would she pay the extra cash to buy a vacant lot, run utilities, pour foundations, and move those row homes if the neighborhood society is willing to fight a legal battle that stands to seriously benefit her? If they secure an injunction that says those houses can't be demolished, then all she has to do is pony up the cash to buy them, and then she can rehab them where they stand. In other words, we'll be screwed. Again."

Leave it to Ethan to make sure the light of doubt still shined squarely on Stuart. "That's not going to happen," he said. "I'll make sure of it."

His father shook his head as he raised the newspaper. "I hope so, son. I really do, because you're down to your last chance."

God, how he hated those words.

Chapter Six

Angie carried a bowl of steaming meatballs to the dining table in her mother's Lawrenceville home. The house wasn't big enough to comfortably fit twenty Corcarellis every Sunday for dinner, but Ma did it anyway—ever since Nonna had passed. Maybe even more touching was that everyone still came. Because family mattered, and when they were together like this, it almost seemed like her dad and Nonna were here, too.

"You're gonna pull her arms out of their sockets," she said to her cousin Vin, who was lifting Tony and Trish's little girl, Angelina, by the arms like a human bungee cord.

Vin rolled his eyes. "When was the last time you heard of that happening? Man rips child's arms out of socket—full story at eleven." He lifted Angelina and blew a noisy kiss against her neck while she giggled. "Your Aunt is a fearmonger."

Tony, that little shit, laughed, too.

"Hey," Angie said, slapping the bowl to the table. "You laugh while I'm trying to keep your kid safe. How warped is that?"

"Oh, so we're talking warped now, huh? Then let's talk about Stuie showing up at your place last night."

If anything warranted a "screw you" that was it, but never in front of her innocent niece.

"Yeah, that was surprising, wasn't it?" Trish asked as she followed Aunt Connie into the dining room, both of them carrying more food.

Uncle Gene skirted the table, leaning over bodies so he could pour the wine. "Who's Stuie?"

"You dating someone, Ange?" Vin asked.

"No!" But that damn kiss made it so she couldn't look Trish in the eye.

"Jo, I forgot the extra sauce," Ma said. "Can you grab—"

"I got it," Angie said, practically knocking Aunt Jo down as she lunged for refuge in the kitchen.

She loved her family enough to let them dictate most of her life down to her profession, but she wasn't going to get dragged into a conversation about Stuart Perrault.

The minute her hand wrapped around the gravy boat filled with meat sauce, someone walked into the kitchen and opened the refrigerator.

That didn't mean she was going to have to talk about Stuart. She turned around and came face to face with Trish.

"Hey." She lifted the gravy boat and gave a guilty shrug. "Can never have too much sauce at a Corcarelli dinner."

Trish nodded as she unscrewed the top of a sippy cup. "Are you okay?"

"Yeah. Fine."

"You seem off."

"Nope."

"Did something …" she filled the cup with milk, "bad happen with Stu?"

That depended on how you defined bad.

Trish returned the milk to the top shelf and shut the refrigerator door with her hip. "I mean, I know how important those houses are to you, and I know how stubborn Stu can be when it comes to business. I just don't want this battle to hurt you."

"Not possible," she said, adding a snort and squaring her shoulders. Life had beaten the shit out of her between her father's early death and her grandmother's battle with ovarian cancer, and still, she was standing. If anyone was in danger of being hurt, it was Stuart with that damn silver spoon in his mouth. One good push, and he'd choke on it.

"Angie, where's the fricking sauce?" asked Vin in a bellowing voice that carried in from the other room.

She was happy to get away from this conversation—the conversation she'd tried to get away from when she'd fled to the kitchen in the first place. This family was relentless, and Trish fit right in.

"Ange?"

She glanced at Trish over her shoulder. "Yeah?"

"Stu isn't the kind of guy to show up unannounced late at night unless he has something important to say. Last time he did that to me, he was there to reconcile, only your brother was there to greet him." She cringed. "I guess what I'm trying to say is if you need to talk about whatever is going on, I'm here."

Angie nodded. "I know." But knowing Trish was here and that she suspected something was going on only increased the pressure to finish this fight so Stuart Perrault could go back to being a non-issue between them.

"Is everything okay?" Ma stood in the doorway.

That seemed to be the question of the day. "Fine," Angie said, forcing a smile.

"We were talking about the houses," Trish added.

"The houses on the news last night?"

Angie nodded and pushed past her mother. "Vin needs his sauce."

And for the first time in her life, she felt like she needed some distance from her family.

"It's about damn time," Vin said when she finally reached the dining room.

She ignored him and sat.

"Ange, you got room for Enzo on your crew?" Uncle Gene asked. "He needs to quit that restaurant. I told him no self-respecting man should be waiting tables. Build something."

She didn't have room. She was barely making payroll for the family she already carried. But looking at her teenage cousin, who was staring at his plate, she sighed. She couldn't say no to her family. They came first.

"Enz, do you want to learn construction?" she asked.

He shrugged. "Yeah. Pop would like that."

Like her pop had liked it when she and Tony had wanted to learn alongside him.

"Okay," she said. "Then you give your notice at the restaurant, and you come see me on Friday when I'm in the office. We'll get you settled."

"Thanks."

"Speaking of coming to see you." Tony reached across the table for the breadbasket. "Are you ever going to tell us what happened last night after we left?"

"No."

"Ooh! What happened last night?" Aunt Jo asked.

"I wanted to punch some smug bast … guy," Tony said.

"Now you've got to tell the story, Ange," Vin said. "You can't leave us hanging."

"Okay. Okay." She would just skip the part about the kiss. It wasn't really important anyway. It was a heat of the moment kind of thing. It wasn't like she had to worry about it leading to Stuart sitting across from Tony at Sunday dinner. She crossed her arms to stop a shudder.

That was never going to happen.

In fact, as far as she was concerned, she had no reason to speak to or see Stuart Perrault again. He could take his idea for her to buy and move the properties and shove it up his ass.

Great. Now, she was thinking about his ass.

• • •

By Thursday, Stuart had almost forgotten about the lapse in judgment that led him to that kiss. Almost. He only remembered it every time he opened his mouth.

"Simon Cross is on line two," his secretary's voice prompted from the speakerphone on his desk.

"Thank you." He hit the flashing red button. "Simon, how are you?"

"I'd be better if these people weren't moving forward with this baseless case."

"I'd be better, too." Because his father wasn't letting up.

As much as Stuart felt it was wise to stay away from Angie, his father was pushing him toward her and this new deal, which was Stuart's idea in the first place. Idiot.

"So, your message was, hypothetically speaking, could those houses be moved to another lot? The answer is yes, but there's no guarantee they'd survive the move. That end unit can't be entered it's so dangerous. Honestly, I don't know how it could be stabilized. But if someone were willing to lose that one to save the other two, it would be doable. Expensive, but doable."

"My rough estimate for the move alone, not including permits, is one hundred grand." He'd spent a good portion of the week making contact with people who could guide him.

"You're not considering doing this are you?"

"No." But he might have to, because if Angie refused to play the game, buying and moving the properties on his own might be the only way for him to save face with his father. He had no idea if that was even morally acceptable. Someone was bound to cry conflict of interest.

He was screwed.

When he'd hung up the phone and turned his attention to the computer screen, a knock sounded on his door.

"Come in."

Ethan poked his head around the doorjamb. "We ordered lunch. You should join us."

And deal with more lectures and disapproving glances. No thanks. "I'm actually heading out. I need to be onsite."

"Problems?" Ethan asked, and then he smiled. "I mean more problems than what we already have?"

"No. Solutions." He grabbed his jacket off the back of his chair, opened the door, and left his brother to lunch with their father.

The ability to come up with solutions under pressure was the hallmark of a business leader. It was a thought that stayed with Stuart on his drive through town. Unfortunately, his best solution was a long shot when it hinged on moving buildings like this.

He walked around the perimeter of the caution-taped properties, stopping to stare at the crumbling foundation and splintering wood of the building Simon said wasn't able to withstand a move.

There wasn't a way to keep everyone happy, was there?

"If you think for a minute that torching it will get you what you want, think again."

He turned to see Angie staring at him from the front corner of the house, and for a second, the harsh words were outshined by the beauty of her face and the memory of her mouth on his. God, she did something to him—something he was afraid to admit.

"If you think for a minute I'd be capable of something like that, then it's no wonder you're out for blood," he said.

She walked toward him. He sort of wished she would keep her distance.

"I'm not out for blood, Stuart. Just these houses." She stopped, leaving plenty of space between them. Apparently they could agree on that. "I have nothing to do with this lawsuit. Nothing. I heard from Maddy it was filed, though."

"There's no guarantee a judge will even hear the case."

"I'm feeling pretty good that one will."

"Okay, say your friends win an injunction and the demolition is panned. Say the city backs off the highway project and puts this property on the sale block. Say you're the winning bidder. You get to rehab these houses right here on this land. It's what you want, right? Then what?" He pointed to the biggest, baddest crack in the foundation. "Will you lift them and pour a new foundation to start?"

She blinked as she stared at the cement block. "Sure. I suppose. I haven't really thought about it."

She hadn't thought about it? He clenched his teeth. She was messing with his future on a whim. "Don't you think you should've ironed out the details before you threw your hat into this ring?"

"Oh, yes, absolutely." Her words dripped with sarcasm. "I should've made some lists. Weighed the pros and cons, right? And missed my opportunity because I was too busy debating whether or not it *was* an opportunity. No thanks. I'll leave that sort of thinking to you."

His jaw ached from holding back. "What about that?" He pointed at the gaping split where the walls were pulling away from each other. "Will you rebuild or repair?"

Her eyes widened as she scanned the house. "I will decide how to proceed once I'm the owner and have the right to make the decisions."

"So until then, you'll just screw me."

They were words. His context was innocent. But her eyes widened even more, and if he wasn't mistaken, a slight blush crept over her cheeks.

"I don't know what you think you're doing," she said.

He shook his head and raised his hands in a surrendering apology. "I'm not ... I didn't ... I ... I came here because I was hoping there was a way for both of us to win. I've been working on the moving idea all week. I'm serious about helping you with that, Angie. I'm not trying to ..." *screw you*? He almost laughed, because memories of that damn kiss wouldn't completely leave his mind. "I'm not trying to hurt you."

She looked away. He wished to God he could do the same, but even firmly positioned as his rival, he was drawn to her.

"Fine," she said. "They're in bad shape, but how does moving them change that? Considering their condition is moving them even possible?"

"The other two, yes. This one? I don't know."

"Even if I decided it was worth the risk of losing one, I can't imagine how much it would cost."

"At least a hundred grand."

She glanced at him.

"I've been doing some research." For her. For him. Because damn it, for some reason he couldn't cut whatever strings were there and throw himself into burying this threat in the first place. "Angie, if the injunction is granted, another developer could swoop in and outbid you anyway, and then we both would lose. But, if we get your offer to buy and move the properties accepted before the court date, then you're guaranteed to get the houses. Just not the property. You could live with that, couldn't you?"

"I don't know, Stuart."

"I do. Trust me on this. I'm willing to put everything I've got behind you, including those lists you make fun of. With proper planning this can work. Let me prove it to you."

She looked pained. But even with a furrowed brow and twisted lips, she was gorgeous.

"Why are you really doing this?" she asked.

For all the wrong reasons. That was for sure. Any way he looked at it, his thinking was warped. Was he doing this because it was his best shot at proving his level of commitment to his father and keeping this project on track, or was he doing this because he liked her and hoped that by helping her she'd come to like him?

Man, that kiss told him he had one hell of a shot.

"I already told you," he said. "I want us both to win."

She shook her head. "But why? Business is business, right?"

"Maybe this isn't just business." The slightest uptick in his heartbeat told him he'd hit the nail on the head. "Angie, you have to know all the lists in the world couldn't have prepared me for that kiss."

She hung her head and dug the toe of her work boot into the ground. "Please, tell me you did not make a list about that."

He smiled. "I didn't. And that's the problem. That's completely unlike me. I don't know what to do about it." He stepped toward her and she looked up. "You make the cons look good."

She stepped back. "We shouldn't be working together or talking about … this. Separate sides. Winner takes all."

"Probably the smart way to handle it."

"Absolutely." But she didn't look convinced. Her face softened, and her lips parted until he could see the tip of the tantalizing tongue he'd tasted. "Tony hates you."

"Yeah, well, the feeling is mutual."

"You wanted to marry my best friend."

"A long time ago." And right now, he couldn't remember why he'd been so hell-bent on spending his life with someone who'd never made him feel this way.

"Stuart."

"Angie." He smiled. "Don't you think we're kind of good together?"

"No." But then her lips quirked, too.

"It was a good kiss, wasn't it?"

"Average."

"Then why are your cheeks pink."

She glared at him. "I'm Italian. My skin doesn't do pink."

In some places he bet it did. Her tongue. Her lips. Maybe her nipples and between her …

"I want these houses," she said. She looked up at them with reverence.

God help him, he wanted her with the same intensity.

"Then, let me help you get them."

"Fine." She glanced at him. "But no funny business."

Agreed. There was nothing funny about this.

Chapter Seven

"Where are you?" Enzo's voice sounded higher on the phone than it did in person. "I'm in front of the office building, but the doors are locked. You told me to come by Friday, right?"

Shit. Angie glanced around the coffee shop she'd spent the better part of the day in. "Yeah, yeah. I'll be right there."

"Problems?" Stuart asked. His blue eyes shined over the rim of a white cardboard cup, and for a minute, her mind blanked.

That was the problem.

"I forgot my cousin was coming to sign some papers today."

"So, we're done for today?" He set down his coffee and closed his laptop.

"We are." She nodded as she stood. "Sorry."

"No problem. We made some headway on the plan. We'll just have to get together again to finish the official proposal for you to buy the row homes."

She scowled even though her pulse quickened. She didn't need to be spending *more* time with him.

"Don't look so thrilled," he said with a laugh that crinkled the skin around his eyes in an alarmingly handsome way.

"I'll, uh, call those banks on Monday." She backed toward the door.

She had a purpose for being here, and it wasn't enjoying a cup of coffee while she ogled Stuart Perrault.

He stood, too, and walked the trash to a nearby bin. "Sounds good. Will you be working on the house tonight?"

His question stopped her at the door. "What house?" And then it hit her. The Popsicle stick house. It was Friday. She'd spent some portion of three Fridays in a row with him.

"The model house," he said. "I'm free tonight if you need some help."

Okay. But she dug her nails into the palm of her hands and refused to let the word slip out. "I have other plans." With her mother. Technically, they could be cancelled. *What?* Why would she cancel on her mother? God, what was wrong with her?

"Ooh," he teased. "Hot date?"

"With my mother. I'm a barrel of Friday night excitement."

He grinned. "I bet you have your moments."

Heat climbed her neck and onto her face. There would be none of those moments with him. Trusting him to help her get these row homes was bad enough.

"Well, since you're busy tonight, I guess I'll have to find another hot date." He lifted his leather bag to his shoulder and fell into step beside her.

Did he kiss all his dates goodnight the way he'd kissed her last Saturday night? *Don't think about this.* She should ignore him when he crossed the line into personal territory. Keep it focused on business.

He pushed the door open and held it for her. "Where did you park?"

"Around the corner." Not far, thank God. She needed to get to her truck, hit the locks, and get away from this man.

Two steps from the coffee shop, and he was still beside her. Must've parked in the same general area. Great.

"Did you build with Legos as a kid?"

That was personal, but random. She squinted against the sun for a better look at him. "Of course, who didn't?"

"Exactly. After seeing you working on that house, I started thinking about the early building influences in my life, and Legos came to mind. I had a ton of them. Still do. Boxes full at my parents'. My mother thought it would be nice to save them for my kids." He laughed. "You know, if I ever get around to having any.

But, now I'm thinking, why wait? Why not get all those Legos and find a truckload more and start a young builders' program in at-risk neighborhoods. It could be an extension of Build Together Pittsburgh."

"Build Together Pittsburgh Kids," she said. "That's an awesome idea."

"I'm glad you think so, because I'd like you to help me with it."

Me? She stopped, looked at him, and then walked on when he stopped, too. Again, she did not need to be spending more time with him. But what a killer idea. "Don't you think we have enough to do already?"

"Nah. Besides, I like spending time with you."

Loaded words. She should hop into her truck and take off without acknowledging them, but she turned and saw his beautiful smile and melted. "I'll think about it ... because it really is a great idea."

He nodded. "Not because you like spending time with me, too, though?"

Don't answer that. But she couldn't seem to stop herself from tossing him a grin as she climbed into her truck.

"You like me, Angie Corcarelli, I can feel it."

Like him? Absolutely. One-hundred-percent trust him? No way. Still ... he wanted to start a nonprofit to encourage kids to build. How bad could he be?

If she were a smart woman, she wouldn't put herself in the situation to find out.

• • •

By the time Angie reached the brick building that held the Corcarelli Carpentry Company offices, the weather had turned, and it was raining. Enzo was soaking wet, sitting on the edge of the sidewalk.

"Why didn't you go home?" she asked, running toward the door with keys in hand.

"Pops dropped me off. Besides I didn't want to look like I flaked out on you. I can do this job, Ange. You guys work in the rain. Well, I can get wet, too." He grinned.

Damn kid. He was too cute. She pushed him inside and grabbed an abandoned sweatshirt off the coat rack and threw it at him. "Put that on before you catch your death."

"Nonna used to say that."

Her heart pinched. "Where do you think I got it?"

He nodded, and when he poked his head through the sweatshirt said, "I miss her."

Me, too. But the best she could do was to swallow the onslaught of tears.

Once the paperwork was filled out, she walked him through the back room to the workshop, trying to get a handle on his knowledge of construction and tools. He was green. Definitely greener than she'd been at his age. Eighteen? Hell, she oversaw her first residential project at eighteen. It was her aunt's kitchen remodel, but still.

"I've got a lot to learn." He grabbed a hammer off the workbench and strangled it.

"You're telling me." She reached for her own hammer. "Hold it like this. Don't choke it. The end is where you'll get a feel for it." She swung the tool, hitting the wooden table with a satisfyingly solid blow. "See? Balance. That's the key."

"Balance." He swung like a drunken lumberjack.

"We'll work on it. That's what apprenticing is for." That and cheap labor. She was almost happy he was clueless. If she had to pay him a standard wage, she'd be screwed.

Damn it. That word was a one-way thought train back to Stuart. And that kiss. And what could happen after another kiss.

"You okay?" Enzo asked.

"Yeah. Of course."

"Your face is really red."

"It's hot in here. You'd think so too if you weren't soaking wet."

"Yo, anybody home?" Tony's voice filtered into the garage.

"Back here," she called.

"Whoa! What the hell happened to you?" he asked when he laid eyes on Enzo's crazy wet hair.

"She forgot about me," the kid said.

"I did not …"

"Uncool," Tony said. "What could be more important than making your cousin an official member of the crew?"

She knew he was trying to make Enzo feel good, but he was annoying the crap out of her.

"Yeah! What he said."

And now the kid was annoying her, too.

"I had something important to do."

"Trouble with one of Trish's projects?" Tony asked.

"No."

Tony's face crinkled. "You were wasting your time on those row houses again."

"Those houses aren't a waste of time. Besides, it's none of your fricking business where I was. Why are you here anyway? It's not like you work here."

"Hey, let's not start that." He held up three stain swatches. "I'm running errands for the pregnant lady. These are for the Kittleman kitchen. Trish said to tell you she wants to see each one on a larger palette. *Please.* The politeness is from Trish, not me, especially after that last jab."

Angie reached for the swatches, but Tony yanked them away. "Not everybody wants to be a carpenter, Ange. You can't keep holding it over my head. Look, you've got fresh blood right here." He punched Enzo's arm. "Maybe I should give these swatches to you, Buddy. It can be your first project."

But Tony sure as hell wouldn't stick around to help the kid with it.

"He doesn't even know how to hold a hammer. Give those to me." She snatched the wood from her brother's hand.

She just wanted him to leave. Between the row house topic, which led straight to Stuart, and Tony's lack of participation in the family business, she didn't feel like small talk.

"So how's it looking down there?" Tony asked.

"Where?" She had three active projects for Trish. She couldn't begin to guess which one he was talking about.

"Hazlett Street."

Ugh. He wasn't going to give up, was he? "Fine."

"Ma says there's a full-fledged lawsuit now."

Of course her mother went ahead and spread that around. The woman's telephone was glued to her ear.

"Yep. Not that I had anything to do with filing that. But, a judge could order a halt to the demolition." If things worked out like Stuart planned, there'd be no need for that, though. She'd buy and move the houses, bringing this all to the most peaceful end possible.

"Beautiful." Tony smiled. "I love seeing Stuie lose."

For crying out loud, this was getting old. Tony got the girl. "Stuart," she said.

"Huh?"

"Just … his name is Stuart. Stuie is stupid."

"*Par. Done. Me.* I didn't realize you had a preference." His face twisted, like he was sitting under an interrogation spotlight. "You do have a preference, don't you? That's why the loser showed up at your house at midnight last Saturday night."

"Stop it, Tone."

"Holy Christ. Does my wife know you're messing with her ex?"

"No! Wait." Did he know about the kiss? He couldn't know. "What are you talking about?" *Deny, deny, deny.* "There is nothing to know. Stuart and I are tangled up in this highway mess. That's it."

He didn't look like he believed a word she'd said. "Come on." He wrapped a hand around Enzo's bicep. "I'll give you a ride home."

"You're being an idiot," she said.

He didn't even turn around.

"Thanks for the job, Angie." Enzo followed Tony out the front door.

What just happened here? She whaled the hammer against the workbench and let out a roar. Tony couldn't possibly know about that kiss. She hadn't told anyone—yet. She was going to have to come clean to Trish, wasn't she? Tony would rant about it to his wife, and he'd get it all wrong, wrong enough that he could have Trish thinking the worst. Angie wasn't sleeping with the guy. Absolutely not.

Whatever prompted that kiss was basic biology messing with two single people. It wasn't a crime. Sleeping with him wouldn't be a crime either, but it would cross a line. Wouldn't it?

She told herself the kiss, the thoughts, and the feelings were no big deal as she drove to Trish's interior design showroom. The business was housed in a gorgeous brick building on the swankiest street in Shady Side. Angie always felt a dime short and ridiculously underdressed when she walked into the place.

"Hey," Trish called out the instant she saw her.

"Hey."

"Did you get the swatches?"

"Yep." Angie smiled. That floral dress could only work on a pregnant Trish. Anyone else would look like she was wearing curtains. "This stomach has the last one beat."

Trish patted the bulge and then turned to pull some fabric off a nearby bolt. "You always show sooner with the second."

She wouldn't know. Not that she didn't want to know. She just didn't see how kids could fit into her life. Too many people were depending on her already. She couldn't very well climb a ladder when she was nine months pregnant, or strap a newborn to her chest while she cut lath. And there was nobody else to trust with the carpentry company. Hell, her father had tried that with Tony. If her brother could look a dying man in the eye and say he wasn't interested in running the family business—even temporarily, he sure as heck could look his pregnant sister in the eye and say the same thing.

"So, what's up?" Trish asked.

Was it too late to play this off like a random visit?

"I kissed Stuart."

Or she could just blurt it out like that.

"Actually, he kissed me, but I kissed him back, and you should know why, because … you kissed him first."

The fabric slipped from Trish's hand and puddled onto the desk. "Seriously? But you hate him."

"Apparently not. I mean, he's still not my favorite person in the world, but my body seems to be able to look past that."

"Huh." Trish stared off into space. "Of all the scenarios I imagined of what was going on between you two, that was last on my list. I mean, it was on my list, especially after Saturday night, but … huh," she said again. "I didn't really think you could get past your hatred."

Me neither. "You can go ahead and be mad at me. I won't blame you. Like I said, you had him first." And *that* was gross. She couldn't even think of that. All the times she'd made fun of Trish and Stuart's vanilla sex life. Ugh. What was she doing even having this conversation?

"I'm not mad at you or Stu. I'm happily married, Angie. I see no reason why you can't pursue him if you want to. I'm just surprised either one of you would pursue the other while you're on opposite sides of this highway project. That's so unlike him. He's a very deliberate, careful person."

That's what she'd thought, until he kissed her. "We're not actually on opposing sides anymore. I mean, I still want the houses, and he still wants the highway, but he thinks he's figured out a way for us to both get what we want."

"Interesting."

"Is it? Because crazy seems like a better word to me. I still don't know how I'm supposed to trust him."

"With the row homes or your heart?"

Gag. This conversation was getting more uncomfortable by the minute. "If Tony finds out about that kiss, he will blow a gasket."

"So don't tell him. We didn't tell you about us when we first started messing around."

"Thank God."

"Well, what's good for the goose and all that."

"But he already suspects something. If he asks you outright, are you going to lie to him? He's your husband now. You'll choose him over me. I know you will."

"He's not going to ask. He'd rather be in blissful denial than hear there's something actually going on."

"There's nothing actually going on."

Trish grinned.

Angie growled. "It was one kiss."

"Whatever it was or wasn't or is or isn't, don't worry about Tony. He'll survive."

"I'm not worried about him surviving. I'm worried about Stuart."

Trish's grin widened. "That's sweet."

"No, it's not. I just don't want blood on my hands."

"And here I thought you were telling me this so I'd give you my blessing to date him."

No, no, no. Angie shook her head. "I'm telling you this so my conscience is clear. Stuart is not the man I should be messing around with."

"But your body thinks otherwise. You said so yourself."

"Forget what I said. I'm not going to piss my brother off even more and take a stab at your leftovers simply because I'm horny."

Trish laughed. "Angie, I really don't care."

"I do."

"Then get over it. Stu's a good guy. You're a good woman. You both like to build things. It could work."

As in long term? That was a joke. A lifetime of Popsicle stick houses, truckloads of Legos, and charity builds sounded sweet, but she needed more. Like a passionate man, not a risk-analysis obsessed paper-pusher. What if that kiss was a one-time deal? And what about his uptight family? "Can you see me lunching with his perfect parents?"

"You manage with mine."

"Your mother almost choked on her *coq au vin* when I dropped the f-bomb at dinner."

Trish laughed. "Look how far she's come. She loves you now!"

"Because I built her a breakfast nook. Besides, my brother impregnated you. She probably figured she didn't have a choice. And even if Stuart's parents were cool, can you imagine Tony sitting across the dinner table from Stuart without wanting to leap across to pulverize him? He's territorial. He'll never believe Stuart doesn't want you."

"Is that what you think?"

The bell above the door rang, and they both looked at the woman striding toward them.

"Hello, Mrs. Collingsworth," Trish said. "I'll be right with you."

That was Angie's cue to leave, and the perfect way to avoid Trish's question. But it followed her to the sidewalk. How long ago had Stuart and Trish broken up? Trish and Tony's little girl was three. It took a year for her to bake, and Stuart had lived in Paris two years before that. Six years? A long time ago. Enough to fall out of love and move on. And yet, three years ago, he'd shown up on Trish's doorstep ready to rekindle things. What if Tony hadn't been there?

She growled. *Pointless.* This whole train of thought. It was a kiss, not a proposal. Forget about it. And if by chance it happened again, it would just be a kiss again.

Not that she was hoping for that.

Chapter Eight

Stuart pulled a bottle of pinot noir off the wine rack and set it on the granite countertop.

When was the last time he'd had a woman besides his mother over to his house? Trish? She was definitely the last woman who'd been in his bed. God, that seemed like a lifetime ago. Maybe that was why he was so out-of-his-mind around Angie. He was long overdue for some quality time with a woman.

But he was getting ahead of himself. Angie had only agreed to meet him in order to finish the proposal for purchasing the row homes. Still, he couldn't help but smile, because she had agreed to come here, and here was much cozier than a coffee shop.

He popped the cork from the bottle and sniffed the red-tipped end. The oaky, current-heavy scent woke him up a bit. What was he doing? Angie drank beer. Besides, this was supposed to be a business meeting. He didn't want to run her off.

After corking the bottle, he put the glasses away, and a minute later, the doorbell rang. A kick in his heart rate sent him jogging toward the door. He stopped, took a deep breath, and walked the rest of the way. He was not the kind of man who ran to answer the door under any circumstances.

When he opened the door, he found her wearing a tiny T-shirt, fitted jeans, and a smile that made her worth sprinting halfway around the world for.

"Hey," she said.

"Hello." He hoped his grin didn't look as predatory as it felt. "How are you?"

Her eyes shifted as she looked around the exterior of his house. "Impressed. Is this an actual Frank Lloyd Wright?"

"Nope. It's only inspired by the greatest architect who ever lived."

"Michelangelo is the greatest architect who ever lived."

"Of course you would think that. Why am I not surprised?"

"That I'd choose Michelangelo over Frank Lloyd Wright, or that I'd disagree with you?"

"Both." He chuckled as he stepped aside and waved her into the house. "Regardless of your misguided opinion on the ranking of architectural greats, I'm glad you like my house. Let me show you the rest of it."

"Should I take off my shoes?"

"No. The floor is slate, and it's miserably cold because there's no radiant heat."

She looked down at the floor or maybe her feet. He couldn't tell exactly, because her dark hair hung forward blocking his view. "Are you sure? I don't mind. 'Shoes off' is sort of a requirement in a Corcarelli house. My mother makes us take off our shoes. Nonna used to make us take off our shoes. And now, Trish makes us do it."

She looked up at him then, her brow wrinkled.

"You know, I don't mind when you mention Trish."

Her nose wrinkled, too. "I don't mind mentioning Trish, either. It's my grandmother that stings a bit. She, uh, died … last year. I'm still trying to get used to it."

"I'm sorry about that." But he wasn't sorry that he took the opportunity to state his case about Trish. He didn't want her to be an issue between them.

She nodded and stepped further into the house, sliding a finger along the grout of the brick walls. "How long have you lived here?"

"A few years. I bought it when I returned from France."

"It looks like you just moved in. There's nothing on the walls. What would Trish say?" She gave a tight-sounding laugh.

"I don't care what she has to say." Again. He wanted to make that crystal clear. "I'd rather hear what you have to say."

She studied him. The intensity would be unnerving if it weren't so damn alluring. "Okay, well, I say it's not very cozy." She looked around the room again. "You don't even have a couch. And where's your TV? You don't hang in here, do you?"

"I *hang* in my office mostly. It's down the hall attached to my bedroom. I'll show you if you'd like."

One thin brow lifted, but she cracked a smile. "I'll pass. We have work to do."

He smiled, too, but he'd rather "work" in the bedroom. "Let me show you to the dining room. That's where I left the laptop and the lists."

"Ooh! Lists. Be still my beating heart." She rolled her eyes.

Until her, he'd never found sarcasm the least bit sexy.

When they reached the room between the kitchen and den she shook her head. "That's the smallest dining table I've ever seen."

"It doesn't get much use. I eat—"

"At your desk." She rounded the table and pulled back a chair. "That's … depressing or obsessive or both. And exactly what I'd expect."

"Well, before I was interrupted, I was going to say I eat at the kitchen counter." Was that even more depressing? Probably. He'd never thought about his dining habits before.

"I eat at the counter, too, unless I'm having my family over for dinner. I do that a couple times a month."

Dinner with Tony Corcarelli. He couldn't imagine a meal causing more indigestion. *And yet, here you are, looking to make the moves on his sister. Again, what are you doing, man?*

The answer was simple. He wanted to have sex with her. He didn't want to marry her. Maybe that made him a pig, but at least he was an honest one. Between their past and their current predicament, all it could ever be was sex. He couldn't imagine

Tony accepting him at Sunday dinner any more than his father would accept Angie at Sunday brunch. And that didn't even take into account the awkwardness that would come from being with Angie around Trish.

Fortunately, Angie seemed like the kind of no-rules, non-traditional, impulsive woman who wouldn't balk at such an arrangement … if she were interested. That kiss in front of her house told him there was a good possibility she could at least be persuaded.

He pulled out a chair and sat beside her. "Ready to get down to business?" He should be. Libido aside, there was still a project and control of a company at risk here.

She angled herself toward his open laptop. "Let's get to it."

"Have you seen this before?" He pointed to the screen. "It's the webpage where the city lists all properties for sale." She shook her head. "This …" he clicked on the "Make an Offer" link, "is where they list the worst properties, ones that are hard to valuate. They make it easy on themselves by putting the ball in the contractor's court. It's exactly what it says—you make an offer."

She reached over and nudged his hand off the touchpad so she could maneuver the cursor. The slight contact had his skin buzzing and business focus waning.

"What sort of offers are we talking about here?" She leaned closer to the screen, which showed a picture of a dilapidated foursquare with a gaping hole in its roof.

He could smell her lavender perfume.

"Well …" he set his hand gently over hers and squeezed as he lifted her off the touchpad so he could regain control of the computer. The heat that slashed through him dampened his palms.

Regaining control of the computer was the least of his worries.

He cleared his throat as he clicked to open another document. "I got this from a friend of mine at City Hall. This is a comprehensive list of all city-owned properties sold last year. The ones with an asterisk were sold as 'make an offer' properties. Their sale prices are listed here." He pointed to the far right column. "If we can get the city to agree to list the Hazlett Street properties here, then I think you'll pay a similar price."

"Five dollars? Are you serious?"

"Yep."

This time, when she nudged him out of the way, she did so with her entire body, scooting to the upper right corner of her seat, until she pressed against him. He definitely liked spending time with her like this.

"Was it only a foundation?" Her long fingers flew over the keyboard, calling up the tax assessment website without the need for a search engine. She typed in the house's address, and clicked on the image of a crumbling stone structure located in Troy Hill. "Holy shit," she whispered. "It's amazing." She sat back, staring at the screen. "Five dollars." She shook her head. "*Five* dollars." She exhaled. "Fuck me."

She didn't have to ask twice.

A jolt of something primal and entirely inappropriate had him thinking about kissing her again and getting right down to real business. "Angie?"

She dragged her gaze from the computer and focused on him. "Yeah?"

"You need to watch what you say."

Her face crinkled. "Aw, poor, proper Stuie, did I offend you?"

He wished, because that would've prompted a more comfortable reaction. "You didn't offend me." He leaned closer. "Not at all."

Her eyes widened like she was finally catching on. "Oh. It was just an expression."

"And a suggestion. A powerful one. So ... watch your mouth ... unless ..." He couldn't pull his gaze away from her glistening lips.

She kissed him.

The surprise maneuver left him with eyes wide open for the first couple seconds. But then, she yanked on his collar and opened her mouth over his, and he settled. Head tingling, heart racing, tongues tangling. *Butterscotch.* He smiled against her wet lips. He loved the way she tasted.

But it ended too soon.

"Do you really think I can get those houses for five dollars?" She pulled back so they were nose to nose.

"Maybe less."

"And how much will it cost to move them?"

"I have a chart for that." He turned to look at the computer.

She gripped his jaw and turned him back. "I don't care about your chart." She nipped his bottom lip. "Charts ruin the mood. Just tell me."

Damn. He wasn't going to do anything to ruin this mood. "About $125,000, which includes the land."

She grinned and nipped at his lips again. "I could do that."

Her hands smoothed over his thighs, and he was just about to say "screw it" to the rest of this conversation and haul her off to his bed, when he realized she was getting ahead of herself. Sometimes having a practical mind sucked.

"Don't forget you'll have rehab costs," he said.

"Let me guess; you have a chart for that, too." She slid her hands higher, the tips of her fingers closing in on what was fast becoming an erection.

"I do." He swallowed the moan building in his throat. "But I really don't want to ruin this mood, so I'll just tell you. Probably another hundred grand."

She stilled. "That's pushing it, and that's a lot of money for the neighborhood."

"It is." He slipped a hand to her neck and drew his thumb along her jaw. "But rehabbed row homes a few blocks away are selling for $125,000. Each. And that's exactly the neighborhood you'll be in if you buy one of the vacant lots I've listed in these documents."

Her eyes lit up. "Then, this could work. It could really work."

It could, if everything went off without a hitch. But he wasn't going to focus on that right now. He was going to focus on her.

"We could both end up with what we want out of this, couldn't we?" she asked.

He slipped his other hand to her neck. "That depends on how honest we're willing to be about what we want."

"What do you want?" she whispered.

"I want you." He set a gentle kiss on her lips. "The question is do you want me?"

• • •

Did she want Stuart? Once again, her body was screaming, "Yes, please." And she'd never been very good at impulse control so she gave in, returning her hands to his thighs and leaning in for another kiss. Everything sort of woke up inside of her when they connected. She wanted that rush, for sure.

She let her tongue play with his, let her hands soak in the feel of his hot, hard thighs.

He dragged his lips along her jaw. "Is this your answer?"

Oh, what the hell. "No, this is." She grabbed the hem of her T-shirt and pulled it over her head, then tossed her bra aside, too.

There'd be no doubt of what she wanted, now.

His face flushed, and it was, hands down, the sexiest thing she'd ever seen.

"That's one hell of an answer," he said.

"Yep, so are you just going to sit there staring at me, or are you going to do something about it?"

He grinned. "You're mouthy, but I can be mouthy, too." He leaned forward and lifted her breast to his lips, teasing her nipple with his tongue.

Damn. She sighed and threaded her fingers into his hair while he pulled on her tight skin, making her quiver. Liquid heat pooled between her legs as she watched him move to the other breast.

This was quite the business meeting.

He planted kisses on her chest and over her collarbone until she closed her eyes and dropped her head back, giving him full access to her neck. His warm hands played with her still-damp breasts, and nothing else mattered. It had been so long since someone had taken the time to get to know her like this. *Mmm.* She'd missed it.

Something rattled in the distance, but still his mouth climbed higher, over her chin until he captured her lips. The way he kissed … mind blowing.

What happened in her driveway was not a one-time thing.

More rattling. Through the lusty haze she recognized it as knocking.

Stuart must have, too, because he bolted into an upright position.

"Are you expecting anyone?"

"No." He stood and smoothed out his clothes. "Stay here. I'll see if it's worth answering."

She scrambled into her bra and T-shirt, knowing she looked guilty as sin. Hopefully it wasn't someone worth letting in, because she was pretty sure one look in her direction would give them away.

Maybe it was divine intervention. Probably her dad or Nonna giving her some time to pull her head from her ass and see that this wasn't such a good idea.

Oh god! The idea of her dad or Nonna watching what just happened. She glanced at the ceiling, placed a hand over her heart, and mouthed, "I'm sorry."

"I'm in the middle of a business meeting." Stuart's voice sounded abnormally loud and forceful. "I wasn't expecting any interruptions."

Shit! Whoever it was wasn't going away.

She heard muffled voices getting closer. A woman … and another man.

"We won't stay long," the man said.

Ten seconds later, she was face to face with Stuart's father, whose over-the-top smile could only be described as disturbing. He knew, didn't he? Maybe her face was still red. Was she breathing too hard? And her hair. Had Stuart made a mess of it? She glanced at her shirt to make sure she hadn't put it on backward or inside out, and then she lifted her chin and attempted a smile at both Mr. Perrault and the well-dressed woman behind him.

"Dad, you know Angie Corcarelli from Corcarelli Carpentry Company. Angie, you remember my father, Alan. Well, this is my mom, Mary." His words were clipped, and his eyes were narrowed. He wasn't happy about this impromptu meeting. Either because his parents had interrupted … or he didn't want them to see him with her.

"Good to see you again, Mr. Perrault. Nice to meet you, Mrs. Perrault." She lifted from her seat and held out her hand.

"We were just going over some hypotheticals," Stuart said.

Alan glanced at the laptop. "Anything I can help with?"

Stuart shook his head. "Nope. I've got it covered."

The older man smacked Stuart on the back and then looked at Angie. "What you're doing is very admirable, Miss Corcarelli. Moving historic homes to save them from the wrecking ball? Very admirable indeed. And we're happy to be a part of this philanthropic effort. We support you one hundred percent."

Funny. When he talked about it in his fast-paced, boisterous voice, she didn't feel supported. She felt … manipulated, like she hadn't been given a choice. Either she bought the houses and moved them, or she risked watching them torn down or losing them to another investor once a judge intervened, halted demolition, and caused a firestorm of publicity.

"Thank you," she said.

She couldn't help but glance at Stuart, who was now grinding his teeth together so hard his jaw pulsed.

"Stuart, aren't you going to offer us something to drink?" Mary asked.

"Sorry. I didn't realize you were staying long enough to drink anything, considering we're trying to get some work done."

"There's always time for civilized behavior, darling. I'll take an iced tea. Unsweetened."

"Oh, that sounds good," Alan said.

Angie could barely breathe under the weight of his stare. He pulled out a chair for his wife, and then he sat across from Angie at the too small dining table.

Great. Now he'd be staring her down for God only knew how long. She should leave. Make something up. She was a business owner. Things happened. She could fake a call.

"What about you, Angie?" Stuart asked. "Iced tea, water, soda, vodka?" He stressed that last one, and the corner of his lips twitched.

Or maybe she could stay a little longer. Wait his parents out. Pick up where she and Stuart left off.

"I'm good," she said. Much better after that little moment of commiseration.

"So how's the carpentry business?" Alan asked once Stuart left the room.

"Can't we talk about something else?" Mary asked. "I feel like every time we gather around a table the talk turns to construction. I put up with it at Sunday brunch because I know it's how you prepare for the week, but it's Saturday." She leaned in and tapped

Angie's wrist. "It's nice to have a break from shop talk once in a while, isn't it dear?"

Alan rolled his eyes. "What would you like to talk about, Mary? Shopping, tennis, or manicures? I'm sure a woman who owns a construction company would find those topics infinitely fascinating." He laughed, but the hearty sound didn't override the rude sentiment.

What a jerk. She might have a closet filled with T-shirts and jeans, but she knew her way around a department store. And while she'd never picked up a racket in her life, she could sink a three-pointer with her eyes closed. Fancy manicures were a waste of money for a carpenter, but she should own stock in a hand lotion company for the amount she used.

Bottom line, she wasn't as rough as he was insinuating, and he didn't need to belittle his wife like that.

"I'm sure she would, too," Mary said with a smile. "But I was thinking more along the lines of conversation to get acquainted. Corcarelli? That's Italian, isn't it?"

Angie nodded. "My father was born in Naples. He moved to America when he was a teen."

"It's obvious, dear. You have that beautiful Mediterranean skin. Flawless. I'd pay thousands for a cream that made me look like that."

Ha! She liked this woman. "Thank you very much."

"Two iced teas." Stuart walked into the dining room with a drink in each hand. "What did I miss?" His wide eyes pleaded with Angie.

"Nothing really," she said.

"I wanted to talk business, but your mother preferred something shallower."

Mary took a glass from Stuart and smiled. "Thank you, and don't listen to him. I was simply complimenting Miss Corcarelli on her flawless skin. It really is quite gorgeous. Don't you think?"

Alan twisted so he was facing Stuart, and the back of his head was to Angie. He seemed very interested in his son's response. Angie wasn't, though. There was nothing quite as embarrassing as waiting on a forced compliment.

Stuart didn't even look at her. "I'm a guy, mom. I don't notice those things."

Ouch. Not that she expected more than an unenthusiastic "sure" just to humor his mother. But his quick response shook her. He was different around his parents. That shouldn't have surprised her.

Whatever. Her face may not have impressed him—her breasts sure had.

"You two are ridiculous," Mary said. "Honestly, my husband and sons don't appreciate beauty unless it's made of cement and steel."

"I prefer wood," Angie said. "It's much warmer."

Mary batted her lashes and sighed. "You're going to pass excellent genes onto your babies someday. Lucky's the man who snags you."

Stuart groaned. "Leave the woman alone, Mom. She's here to discuss real estate, not … that stuff."

"What a shame," Mary said.

Alan grinned like a gremlin.

Uncomfortable didn't even begin to describe this conversation, and that was saying something. She was of childbearing age in a family who lived for pregnancies and births. She'd weathered enough questions about when she'd get married and start a family that this should be a piece of cake. Mary was giving her compliments after all. But with Stuart fidgeting at the other end of the table, refusing to make eye contact with her, and his father making enough for the both of them, this was painful.

Hooking up with Stuart wasn't worth it. If she wanted sex bad enough, she could find it someplace less complicated, where the guy didn't have carnal knowledge of her best friend and her brother didn't hate him, and where the guy's mother wasn't so eager for grandkids, and his father wasn't a creep. And where the guy didn't warp into some weird shell of who he'd been when his parents came sniffing around.

Face it. No matter how much her body wanted Stuart Perrault, she didn't belong with him.

Chapter Nine

There wasn't anything Stuart could've said to make Angie stay. He was surprised she'd stayed as long as she had. Honestly, after his mother's desperate attempts to bring Angie to his attention as a possible baby maker, he wasn't in the mood to pick up where they'd left off anyway.

"What a nice young lady," his mother said. "And she's in construction, too. You don't find that every day."

"Please, stop." He gathered the empty glasses and carried them into the sink.

She followed him. "Stuart, you're being silly about this. All I want is for you to be happy. You know, there's more to life than work. You haven't dated anyone since Trish. That worries me."

God, he hated conversations like this. Mostly because he knew she wasn't having these conversations with Ethan. Ethan had a different date every weekend night. If he could figure out a way to tactfully get his mother more interested in Ethan's potential for contracting STDs, he sure as hell would.

"You're wrong, Mom. I date."

"Well, not regularly enough to introduce us to anyone."

"Because you'll start pointing out her childbearing hips, and breasts that were made for nursing."

She swatted his arm. "I would not do that." She chuckled. "I'm more discreet."

"Barely." Still, when he looked at her, he couldn't help but smile. She was the only loving member in his highly competitive family.

"Mary, are you ready?" His father stood in the doorway.

"I suppose." She smacked a quick kiss to Stuart's cheek. "Think about it."

Out on the front stoop, his father turned to him and shook his hand. "Well done, son."

He was puzzled. "What did I do?"

"I think you know."

"Don't forget brunch tomorrow," his mother called from the passenger side door.

He nodded, smiled, and then turned his attention back to his father. "No, I don't know."

"I'm not a dummy, son. I know what we walked in on. It was written all over her face." He chuckled. "She's smitten. Wrapped around your finger. You're calling the shots, boy. And I couldn't be prouder." His hand landed hard on Stuart's upper arm. "See you tomorrow."

Great, he'd made his father proud, but for such a sleazy reason. His father actually thought he was messing around with Angie as a means to keep her under his thumb? Unreal. And yet, he hadn't refuted it. His father's approval wasn't easy to come by. Besides, what would it hurt if he neither confirmed nor denied it? As long as he knew the truth. Right? It wasn't like his mother's wishful thinking would come true.

He needed to pull back. Keep it professional. It would save Angie and him both a lot of aggravation.

The next morning, when he pulled into his parents' driveway for Sunday brunch, Ethan was behind him with the convertible top down. The bass from Ethan's speakers rattled Stuart's rearview mirror. His younger brother was a piece of work.

"Hey, bro," Ethan said as he jumped out of the sports car without opening the door. "Gorgeous morning, isn't it?"

The bastard had gotten lucky last night, hadn't he?

Stuart bit his tongue. "It is."

"Definitely looking brighter than last Sunday, huh? No dooming headlines about the highway project. No angry dad."

"True."

"He's awfully favorable toward you right now." Ethan leaned against his car. "He called me late last night. Got me out of bed." He bobbed his brows and tossed a shitty grin. "Told me not to get Louie involved yet."

Stuart lifted his chin. "Louie?"

"My buddy Louie Carmichael. He would be an excellent candidate for buying and moving those row homes."

"Louie the slum lord?" He could barely get the words out with his tightening jaw.

Ethan laughed. "Come on, now. Louie, the real estate genius who's making millions off stupid college kids who are desperate to rent cheap downtown. There's a difference."

No, there wasn't. "Why would Louie get involved when Angie is ready to make an offer?" But he already knew the answer. His temperature spiked, and he rolled up his sleeves.

"Just a precaution."

"In case I screw up again."

"Don't get bent out of shape."

"Oh, no. Of course not. My father and brother went behind my back to plot against me. What's to get bent out of shape about?"

"Nobody is plotting against you."

"Did you say anything to Louie?"

Ethan shrugged. "Just in passing."

"Perfect." He threw up his hands. "What happens if Louie goes ahead and makes an offer on these properties?"

"I don't know. What's the big deal? All that matters is that those houses are gone so the highway can be built. Who cares who gets the job done?"

Stuart scoffed. "You care. That's what this is about. You can't stand that I'm making progress here. You want to swoop in with your man and your offer and be the savior."

"Oh for crying out loud. You're paranoid, man."

"Am I?" He took a step closer to his brother and stared him down.

Ethan looked away. "We should go in before they come out."

"That's what I thought." He headed for the house. With each step, his blood pressure rose. The games this family played were getting old. He spun around once he reached the garage. "Do you want to run this company and take over for Dad when he retires?" Stuart had never come right out and asked before.

"Do you?"

He pressed his lips together, hating the fact Ethan had turned the question back on him, and struggled just a beat too long for an answer. "That company is my birthright!" *Not yours.*

"That's not what I was asking. Do you *want* to run the company and take over for Dad when he retires? Because I do—even though it's not my *birthright*." He made the gesture for quotation marks in the air, his voice tinged with amusement. "Seems to me the man who *wants* the job more should get it. It shouldn't be given to anyone by default."

Default? Now he was implying that if Stuart became CEO it would be by default and not because of hard work? His blood boiled.

But Ethan wasn't done. "We both know the trouble in Paris happened mostly because you just didn't care enough to stop it," his brother continued. "Dad and I heard about the picketers before you did, and we were an ocean away."

Stuart clenched his hands. "I was in a meeting when the protest happened."

"You ignored the warning signs for at least a month before that. One dinner with the heads of their organization, and you would've seen how serious they were, and then you could've taken appropriate action to stop them; but no. You were too busy hiding behind your desk to—"

"There were deadlines to meet and plans to approve!" He growled. "I didn't have time to care about irrational gossip."

Ethan shook his head. "Exactly. You didn't *care*."

Stuart marched down the driveway until he was in Ethan's face. "Not true. I just underestimated how much other people cared."

Neither one of them blinked.

"Well, to do this job justice—to do any job justice—*you* have to be the one who cares the most," Ethan said. "And in this case, you're not, man."

The words stunned Stuart, and Ethan slipped away.

Didn't care? He'd worked damn hard at this job for the past fifteen years. While Ethan had been out schmoozing clients at three-hour lunches on the corporate expense account, Stuart had been dealing with permit problems and zoning regulations and all the thorny issues with which his brother never bothered to trouble himself. Just because he didn't do his job with a lot of grandstanding didn't mean he didn't care about The Perrault Group. This company was his family's legacy, and yes, Stuart's birthright. He wasn't just going to rollover and let Ethan take that away from him, too.

"We'll see about that," he yelled to his brother's back. And then he added, "May the best man win."

The door slammed behind Ethan, and Stuart stood stock-still. He should put his game face on and follow his brother inside, but what he really wanted to do was leave. Nothing was waiting for him inside that house other than the cold shoulder from Ethan, surface pleasantries from his mother, who would be just as uncomfortable as Stuart, and a father he couldn't seem to please.

The thought gave him pause. Was that the kind of life he had to look forward to as the head of The Perrault Group? Ethan would still be around, claiming he cared more than Stuart did while leaving Stuart to handle all the non-glamorous, thankless details that kept a company running. And their father would never really leave. The man was too much of a control freak to completely disappear. He'd spent so much time at the office over the years, his wife had become a virtual stranger, and still he didn't see the need to cut back on his hours.

Did Stuart even want a life like that?

He blinked.

What a silly question. He'd worked so hard for so long, and of course, this was what he wanted. It was the next logical step in his career path. To throw that away now would be nothing less than foolhardy. What would he do if not this job? He'd never even worked anywhere else.

No, he wasn't about to make a rash, emotional decision like stepping aside just because his brother had gotten under his skin again. Ethan was wrong. Stuart was more than capable of doing the job justice.

He squared his shoulders, lifted his chin, and began the long walk up the driveway to the front door.

Tomorrow, Angie was going to make her offer—if he had to drag her to City Hall himself.

•••

"I want to keep these doors," Angie yelled to her crew, who was scattered around the first floor of a twelve-hundred-square-foot carriage house that Trish's latest client was demolishing in favor of a brand-spanking-new pool house. "These people who destroy history in favor of shiny new bling drive me batshit crazy."

"These people pay my bills," Trish said.

"Yeah, because my stay-at-home-dad, furniture-upholstering, sometimes-artist brother doesn't."

"Don't. He's a good man, Angie."

"Whatever," she muttered and drove the tip of her steel-toed boot into the baseboard. "Keep the woodwork intact, too," she shouted to the crew.

The guys grumbled.

"What's wrong with you?" Trish asked.

"Nothing."

"You're a lousy liar. You've been miserable all morning. Is it the North Side property?"

"No." Although, she was starting to wish she had never driven past those row houses in the first place.

"Then, is it Stu?"

Probably. As much as she didn't want to think about him, she couldn't seem to stop. He'd called twice yesterday and once today. But she didn't want to talk to him. Not yet. What happened at his house on Saturday, from the mini make out session to his parents barging in, was a little more than she wanted to face.

She did not want to face that conversation with Trish, either.

So she walked into the kitchen and examined the cabinetry.

Trish followed. "Angie, look at me."

"Jesus, Trish. Lay off with the chitchat. I'm trying to work here." Not to mention a half dozen Corcarellis were crawling around this place, and she didn't need them overhearing crap about her warped social life. "Enzo, tell Dante I want the crystal pulls and hardware removed, and the wood saved for scrap."

"You got it."

"Morning, Trish."

Angie turned to see Skip Halmark, a local demolition expert, walk into the kitchen.

"Hey, Angie," he said.

She nodded and smiled, thankful she'd get a break from Trish's questions.

"Skip, I'm so glad you could take a look at this for me today," Trish said. "Thank you so much.

"No, thank you." He rubbed a hand across his mouth. "Things are slow. Nobody's knocking anything down anymore, and I've got an extra mouth to feed now, so I appreciate the work."

While Trish and Skip chatted about his new baby and the carriage house demolition, Angie wandered around the empty rooms. *Nobody's knocking anything down anymore.* Was he tapped to knock down the row homes on Hazlett Street? She hoped not. She knew what it was like trying to keep a business afloat when your family depended on you.

With a shake of her head, she refocused. For all she knew some big demo company had been handpicked by the Perraults for that project. She didn't need to go getting all emotional over this.

"She was born with it," Skip said, his voice echoing in the next room. "It's not life threatening, but damn are those medical bills expensive."

Great, he had a sick kid. It was hard not to get emotional over that. She bolted for the front door. *Just get some air.*

Jesse and Giancarlo were carrying a hundred-year-old pedestal sink down the stairs. "Be careful," she said.

"Why's it matter if we gouge the walls, Ange?" Jesse asked in between grunts. "It's getting torn down anyway."

"Don't damage *the sink*, moron. And wrap it before you put it in the truck."

"Ange, some guy is out front looking for you."

She crinkled her face and looked in the direction of her cousin Marco's voice. "Who?"

"He says his name is Stuart."

Shit. Why was he here? How did he know where to find her? He had no business showing up at her workplace ... like she'd gone to him a month ago when she'd driven by the Parkway Extender sign. But *that* was different. It was.

She pushed open the screen door to find him standing on the cobblestone walk dressed in his stuffy business clothes. Except, no tie. His collar hung open, showing off the smooth skin of his throat.

Her mouth watered.

"Hey," he said. "I called Trish's office, and her assistant told me where you guys were working today."

Thanks a lot, Lydia. "You shouldn't be here. Now is not a good time."

"Maybe not, but I need to talk to you. And, you know that already, because I've left three messages saying so. It's important, Angie. Critical, really. I wouldn't have shown up here if it weren't."

She glanced over her shoulder. "I do not want to talk here."

"Then let me take you to lunch."

She looked over her shoulder again at the delivery truck she, Jesse, and Nico had arrived in. Any minute now, they'd bust through the front door with a sink to load. "Fine. But you have to drive. I don't have my truck."

"Great. It will give us more time to talk."

The front door opened, and Skip stepped out. He lifted a hand and smiled. She smiled back, but her guilt flared up.

When she was safely tucked in Stuart's car, she asked, "Who's slated to demo those row homes?"

"Roman Brothers." He glanced at her. "Why?"

"No reason. I was just curious."

And now she could breathe easier, because if she went through with buying and moving the houses, it wasn't like she'd be screwing someone she knew out of work.

"Angie, I'm going to cut to the chase. You need to submit your proposal today. I talked to Simon Cross this morning, and the city is willing to listen."

"But I'm not ready. I haven't called my bank. I haven't talked to Clarisse or anyone from the neighborhood society. I want their blessing, too."

"We don't have time to make it perfect. What we have will have to do."

"Why?"

His face wrinkled. "My brother mentioned the idea of buying and moving the houses to his friend who is also a property investor."

"Who's your brother's friend?"

"Louis Carmichael."

"Are you shitting me?" She glared at him.

"I take it you know the name."

"Yeah, I know the name … and the reputation. That guy is a slimeball. I can't believe your brother is friends with him."

"Yeah, neither can I. But, now you see why it's important for you to make your move today. If Louie is interested, he won't wait."

She was being backed into a corner. With a growl, she faced the window. Were these houses even worth the trouble?

Up ahead on the right, a guy in a Pirates cap was mowing his front lawn. He had a pair of oversized earphones on, and damn it, but that reminded her of her dad. Maybe it was a sign.

"I'll do it, but not until I call my bank," she said.

"How 'bout I take you there and you can talk to someone in person?"

"Fine. I want to talk to Clarisse, too."

"I'll drive you over to the neighborhood society's headquarters as soon as you're done at the bank. And then, we'll head over to City Hall." His hand settled on her thigh, warming the skin beneath her jeans. "The proposal is a good one, Angie. You have nothing to worry about."

Except *that*. She glanced at his hand, noticing the way his fingers curled around her thigh just above her knee.

Nothing about this situation was comforting, and yet, here she was, melting into his leather seat.

Her body was a traitor. Well, at least she had her mind. *Think pushy mom, creepy dad, your best friend, and your brother.* All reasons this hand-to-thigh-action shouldn't matter.

She lifted her leg to cross it over the other, and in the process successfully shed his hand.

Better. Really.

She glanced at him, and he smiled. "Are you nervous?"

About more than she cared to admit. "I don't want to lose to Louie Carmichael."

"I won't let that happen."

Powerful words. Sexy, too. He wasn't even touching her body and her blood was humming.

Pushy mom, creepy dad, your best friend, and your brother.

It wasn't working.

Chapter Ten

Stuart wandered around the lobby of the small storefront used as headquarters for the North Side Neighborhood Society. Black-and-white photos, depicting the area's rich history, hung in precise rows around the gray-colored room that held a desk and a few chairs. Simple, clean lines and masculine colors. He liked the nostalgic feel. But, he didn't like the way his stomach clenched every time his phone vibrated against his hip.

His father and Ethan were looking for him. He'd missed an afternoon meeting. He never missed meetings … until now. But this was important to him. He just couldn't figure out exactly why. Was his desire to best Ethan so strong he couldn't overlook the obvious benefit to the company if absolutely anyone bought and moved the row homes? The project would go off as planned then. Wasn't that what he wanted? Wasn't that what he should be *caring* about?

He heard Angie's laughter in the other room, and he smiled. He still wanted her, too. *Dangerous thinking, buddy.* Emotional thinking. He couldn't risk it if he wanted to stay a step ahead of his brother and Louie.

"Thank you so much for hearing me out." Angie walked into the room with an enormous smile on her face.

Good sign.

Clarisse Young, the association's executive director, stood in the doorway of her office. "Thank you for coming to me," she said. "Best of luck."

When Angie and Stuart were alone on the sidewalk, he said, "That seems to have gone well."

"It did. They definitely want me to have the houses over the city demolishing them, but she warned me opposition to the highway is growing, and they're looking for any legal way to keep the houses on their current land and the highway out."

This could end up a series of court battles—just like Paris.

Before he could get too panicked about that, she pulled her phone from her front pocket. "It's Maddy," she said. "Guess it's time to find out what the Historic Review Commission has to say about this."

He didn't try to keep up when she walked ahead.

His phone buzzed again. A text message this time. From Ethan. *Where are you? Thought you were at the Forbes site, but nobody's seen you there.*

"Oh my God."

He looked up at the sound of her voice to see her coming toward him. *What now?* But she was smiling.

"Maddy said as far as the HRC is concerned they only want the houses preserved. They don't care about the property. That's not their beef."

"So?" He was afraid to sound too hopeful.

"So, a signed bill of sale would halt the lawsuit on their end." She threw her arms around his neck and squeezed. "I could really end up with these houses."

And maybe he could end up with her.

Silly thought. Completely impractical. But with his arms around her waist and his face pressed against her soft, lavender-scented hair, it was a nice thought, too.

"Let me take you to City Hall, where you can drop off the proposal, then later tonight, let me take you to dinner to celebrate," he said.

She released him, but a crooked grin remained. "Are you tired of eating at your kitchen counter alone?"

He grinned. "Maybe. So why not put a lonely man out of his misery?"

"Okay, but on one condition. We go someplace where I can wear jeans and have pizza and beer."

"You got it." Anything to keep him feeling this happy and hopeful.

•••

He was wearing jeans, too. And a sweater vest, but she couldn't fault him for that, mostly because she couldn't stop herself from staring at his denim-covered ass as he stood in line at the bar to order another round of beers. If she ever saw their waitress again, she'd thank her for abandoning them and forcing him out of his seat.

But then a text from Jesse lit up her phone and pulled her attention away.

Sick. Won't be at work tomorrow.

She shook her head. He'd called off work so many times in the last six months she was no longer paying him for missed days.

See a frigging doctor, she typed back. In fact, she'd love a doctor's excuse from now on, because this was getting old … and suspicious. Was he taking advantage of her?

"What's wrong?" Stuart slid a fresh draught in front of her. "Is that about the houses?"

"Nah. It's my cousin calling off work again."

"Oh." He sat. "Does that happen a lot?"

"Too much. It wouldn't be bad if he wasn't the best craftsman I have. When he's gone, his work falls on me." And she already had more than enough to do.

"Because you're the best carpenter in the family, aren't you?"

"Actually, that would be Tony."

Stuart winced, but he raised his glass to his mouth so quickly she nearly missed it. "If that's so, then why doesn't he work with you?"

"When it comes to work, he's a loner." And occasionally a louse, but Stuart didn't need any more reasons to dislike her brother. She was the only one allowed to give Tony trouble for bailing on her and the family business.

"That's too bad."

He looked sincere, but she wasn't buying it. "Really? Are you rooting for Tony now, or are you just a fan of siblings working together because you work with yours?"

"Neither. Your lip hitched when you said Tony was a loner, and I've been around you enough to know that when your lip hitches, it means something isn't making you happy."

She rubbed fingers across her mouth. *Huh.* So much for him not noticing her face.

"I may not be Tony's biggest fan, but it says something about the guy that you'd want to work with him," he said. "My brother and I would be better off working in different companies—on different continents. That says something about him, too."

"You don't get along?"

"We do, but not like brothers, more like friendly business rivals. I can't ever let my guard down around Ethan. I suppose my father is to blame for that. He's been pushing us to compete against each other our whole lives. The earliest advice I can remember from the guy is that only one lion rules the pride."

"Wow." No wonder Stuart was always so driven and serious.

"Yep. And now that Ethan and I are older, it's hard to break that mold. We're still going head to head all the time. And because of that, I'm starting to realize I can't trust him or my father to have my best interest at heart."

Sort of like she struggled to trust him to have her best interest at heart. "Did you tell me about Louie Carmichael and push me to submit a proposal because you didn't want Ethan to win?"

"No. I mean I certainly don't want him to win, but it isn't all about Ethan." Those blue eyes held her gaze with an intensity that made her stomach flip. "It's more about you."

"Really?" Even full-body tingles couldn't squash her skepticism.

"Really." He reached across the table and laced his fingers with hers. "Are you always this distrustful of a man's intentions, or is it just me and mine?"

She looked at their entwined hands, but to her surprise, didn't feel like pulling away. The soft, warm touch comforted her. "In my experience, men aren't very trustworthy."

"Can I ask why?"

"You can ask, but that doesn't mean I'll answer." She grinned and reached for her beer with her free hand.

Then again, maybe she would tell him. He was easy to talk to, and she was tired of holding some of this stuff in.

When she swallowed, she said, "I've loved four men in my life—not counting my extended family members, because even though we're related, I mostly want to throttle them. Five years ago, I loved a man named Patrick, who loved blackjack more than me. Only, I didn't know that until a bookie contacted me to pay his debt. Tony threatened to dismember both men, and my cousin Vin got some law enforcement friends involved." She shrugged. "And that was the end of Pat."

She took another drink. "Before him—way, way, way before him—there was Giuseppe Grimaldi. He was a family friend and an occasional worker on my father's crew. He was almost thirty, and I was in my mid-teens, too young to see what was going on. But my father saw it, and he stepped in. Nobody ever saw the guy again."

"Damn." His eyes were wide.

"Oh, he's alive. Don't worry." She chuckled. "My dad was actually too nice. Giuseppe should've been arrested."

Stuart shook his head. "That's crazy."

"I know how to pick 'em, don't I?" She laughed. "But the sad thing is those guys aren't even the ones who hurt me the worst."

His eyes grew bigger as he reached for his beer.

"Scared, aren't you?" She smiled to hide her insecurity.

"Not at all." He smiled, too. "Okay. Maybe a little."

"Tony is on that list. I love him, but he's kind of a butt when it comes to responsibility. He's gotten better now that he has Trish and Angelina, and that's good. I just can't forget that when our dad was …" she swallowed against the lump in her throat, "dying, he asked Tony to take care of the carpentry company and make sure everyone in the family who wanted or needed a job had a place to work, but Tony didn't want to. He said no. To a dying man. So, I said yes." She blinked back tears. "I have no regrets. I love that company. I do. I just wish I had more help."

He took her hand, and she took a breath.

"And finally, there was my dad. He was the greatest man who ever lived, and still, he let me down by dying way too soon."

"Hey." Stuart tightened his grip. "You can hardly blame the man for dying. I'm sure he didn't want to go."

"No, but it still hurts. Six years later, and every time I climb a ladder I expect him to be holding the rails. When I look down, and he's not, the disappointment kills me. Just once I want to look down and see something that makes me smile." Thinking about it had her throat making funny clicking sounds. "I probably sound nuts. I'm thirty-two. It's not like I need anyone to hold my ladder anymore."

He smoothed his hand back and forth over hers, and smiled. "The ladder's a metaphor. We all want to know someone's there if we need them."

Metaphor? Ha! She'd never dated a man who used a word like that. Not that they were dating. She glanced around the packed bar and then returned her gaze to their hands. Wait a minute. Was this a date?

He slid his hand away from hers, so slowly the warmth lingered. "For what it's worth, I'll be there for you if you need me," he said.

"As far as the houses are concerned, right?

He chuckled. "Doubting my motives again, aren't you?"

She smiled. "Old habits die hard." But more and more she wished that wasn't true.

"I'm not talking about the houses, Angie." There was sincerity in his eyes.

"I know," she whispered, and that scared the crap out of her. She'd gone all these years without a man in her life. Why this one? Why now?

"Let's get out of here. I want to show you something."

She bet he did. Rusty or not in the relationship department, even she knew when things were about to get … interesting.

"Don't look so scared. You'll love it. I promise." He stood, holding out a hand to her. "Trust me."

Tough words to swallow, but tonight, she would sure as hell try.

•••

Stuart looked at the steel structure rising into the night sky and then back at Angie, who was gripping the cold, metal handrails. "You're not afraid of heights are you?"

"Don't you think you should've asked that before you brought me here?"

"Good point." At least someone was making them, because he'd murdered the responsible, practical man inside of him the minute he took her hand in that bar and she hadn't pulled away.

He looked up again. *High.* That's exactly how he felt. And, he didn't want to come down. Not tonight. Tonight, he wanted to be somebody different than he'd been all the nights before. Somebody who didn't worry about the consequences or what his parents would say or if this would get him to the top of anything other than an under-construction skyscraper. He wanted to be somebody who reacted rather than acted. That's why he was here, five stories off the ground, trying to impress a woman he'd always believed to be damn-near unimpressible.

"We could get arrested for this, couldn't we?" she asked.

The higher he climbed, the more wind pummeled his face. "Not likely." He turned his head so she could hear him. "The Perrault Group is overseeing this build, so even though this isn't my project, I have authorization to be here."

"At eleven o'clock at night?"

"Sure. What if my father asked me to check on something?" He hopped off the stairs and onto a platform about sixty-five feet off the ground, where they'd be shielded from the wind by the largest parts of the steel-skeleton frame.

He offered her a hand as she maneuvered over the rail, little more than a shadow in the soft security light.

She took it, and he smiled.

"What about me?" she asked. "Would they arrest me? I don't work for The Perrault Group."

She was close enough that he tasted her on the breeze.

"I'll tell them you're my carpentry consultant."

Skepticism wrinkled her nose. "There isn't any wood around here. It's all cold cement and steel."

Wrong. She was here, and the warmth of her hand in his made him forget about the chilly wind. "Don't focus on that." With an arm to her waist, he turned her around to face the river, where lights from the city, bridges, and stadiums sparkled on the water. "Focus on that." He walked with her toward the open side of the under-construction skyscraper, pressing the front of his body against the back of hers. More warmth. The kind that sparked a flame.

When they were a few feet from the edge, she wrapped both hands around his wrists and pushed against him. "Not too close."

Her worry wasn't lost on him. For all the brash, emotional behavior he'd witnessed from her since the day they'd met at Trish's house almost eight years ago, she was just as scared about making a misstep as he was.

"I've got you," he said, tightening his grip around her waist.

Wind whipped her hair, tossing strands into his face. Chaos. And for the first time in his life, he welcomed it.

"What do you think?" he asked.

Lights from the restaurants high on Mt. Washington peppered the dark shadow on the other side of the river like stars. Views like this were the best part about building bridges and skyscrapers. But after Paris, he'd found himself staring at highway projects. There was no view there … unless he counted her.

He focused on Angie and touched the tip of his nose to the back of her head, losing himself in her.

"It's …" she turned her head, and his lips brushed her cheek. "Amazing."

So true. And not just the view. He splayed a palm against her belly and rubbed the soft shirt against her skin. "You're amazing."

She turned to him, winding her arms around his neck. "You're pretty amazing, too."

Standing here, holding her, the rush was off the charts now.

He kissed her, slipping his tongue into her warm, wet mouth, and letting his body burn. Bits and pieces of the fleshy feast he'd had at his house before his parents had interrupted flashed in his head. He cupped her breasts through her shirt, remembering how they tasted. A few circles of his thumbs around their centers, and they grew hard in his hands.

He was hard, too, straining against the zipper, wanting out, wanting free. "I've never done anything like this," he said as he dragged his lips to her ear.

When he licked, she moaned. "Me, neither."

That made him smile, made him want this even more. It would be a moment they could never forget.

He ran his hands down her arms until he held her hands. "Back here."

Against the concrete shear walls, he lifted her shirt over her head and tasted her again. The soft, salty skin of her neck, her chest, her breasts. He buried his face in her cleavage and breathed. She was the sexiest woman he'd ever seen. The way she clawed his back while she lifted his shirt. The way she pulled his hair while she held his mouth in place.

Don't rush this. He wasn't sure he'd have the guts to do something like it ever again.

She cupped his face and lifted him to her mouth, where she gently scraped his bottom lip with her teeth. It was hot. Wild. He angled his head for a better, deeper vantage point, exploring her mouth with a frenzy, especially when her fingers dipped into the waistband of his pants, and she brushed the taut skin that sheathed his erection.

He hissed.

"We're adding indecent exposure to the trespassing charges," she said, and then she set him free, holding his straining penis in her warm hands.

Damn! Everything about this turned him on. Reckless. Wanton. Sixty-five feet in the air. He'd never done drugs. He'd rarely been drunk. This was higher than he'd ever been.

"I want to fuck you." He breathed the words into her skin.

Her hands stopped moving, and her lips stopped kissing.

He'd crossed a line, hadn't he?

But then she moved again, milking him slowly, brushing her lips back and forth over his. "I didn't know you had words like that in you."

He didn't know it, either.

"I like," she said as she tugged on his bottom lip again only to soothe the sting with a lick. "A lot."

Me, too. "What can I say? You bring out the best in me."

"Like this?" She circled her thumb along the head of his erection.

He growled and spun her around so her back was against the wall. "Like this."

And then he dropped to his knees and yanked her jeans from her hips.

• • •

With her back pressed against the gritty cement wall and the wind in her face, Angie surrendered to the man on his knees. *Stuart.* Part of her felt like she was going to need to confess this. And not because she wasn't treating her body like the temple Sister Clara had always claimed it to be. No, the fact Trish had had him first wouldn't completely let go of her.

But … with his hands kneading her ass cheeks and his tongue pressed against the throbbing flesh between her legs, she was willing to overlook it for now.

"I love the way you taste," he said, never missing a beat with his mouth.

Her knees weakened and opened wider, so she pressed harder against the wall. Sparks of color scattered the hillside, but her vision was too hazy to see details. The only detail that mattered was the soft thrumming of this tongue against her clit. And his finger slipping inside of her.

She whimpered, opening her mouth to breath.

He sucked, and her muscles hardened, wanting to keep him in that perfect place.

"Yes," she hissed.

Two fingers slipped inside of her. The sensations grew.

"Yes," she hissed again.

And with another flick of his tongue, she came. Sliding down the wall on a wave of pure, luscious orgasm.

He caught her, pulled her to stand, and covered her mouth with his. Their tongues tangled as her body pulsed. She could taste the salt of her satisfaction on his lips, and she couldn't imagine anything being sexier. But then his erection pressed against her belly.

She caressed him. Slicked a bead of hot liquid over the velvety skin at his tip.

"Do you trust me?" His voice was low and rough.

She wanted to. After that orgasm, she wanted to believe he could walk on water.

"Yes," she whispered.

"Then put on your shirt but take off your pants."

She obeyed, all the while watching him, holding himself in his hand. Sexy didn't begin to cover that.

"Sit on that ledge," he said.

She hoisted herself up, cringing when the rough surface of the cement scraped her butt, but then he stepped toward her, and in the low light she could see him rolling a condom into place.

The man had one hell of an imagination.

He gripped her around the waist, lifting her slightly and pulling her toward the edge. Again, her butt burned, but she smiled through the sting and wound her arms around his neck for support.

The head of his penis pressed between her folds, and she rocked against him, coaxing new shocks of pleasure from the flesh between her legs. A couple brush burns couldn't compete with that.

"On the count of three," he said against her ear. "One, two ..." And when he ground out three, he lifted her again, so that when she settled into place, she settled right on him.

Mmm. She buried her face in his cologne-drenched neck and reveled in the sensation of his body filling hers. Thick and hard. But the admiration didn't last long.

He backed her against the wall and thrust, pushing the air from her chest on a cry. He thrust again. And again.

It was the most delicious ache. Deep and rigid. Rough and erratic. And with every surge inside of her, he growled.

Stuart Perrault was a gentleman on the street but an animal in the bed? Maybe he was the perfect man.

She captured his mouth with hers, swallowing his next guttural sound. He thrust again, and his broad shoulders tensed beneath her hands. Once more, and she contracted around him, a dull, delicious thumping that she mimicked inside his mouth with her tongue. And finally, he came. Softening around her, pressing his weight against her overheated, over-satiated body.

"Damn," she whispered. "You're a beast."

• • •

He'd lost control. Shedding every inhibition he'd ever had. Caring only about this woman and this act. No one else had ever made him feel strong enough and safe enough to take a chance like that.

Without a damn bit of planning, everything had fallen into place tonight. Everything. The sex was off-the-charts amazing, but it wasn't a purely physical thing. There'd been a connection there, one he wouldn't have with anyone else.

Because Angie Corcarelli was the woman for him.

His heartbeat quickened. He wanted a shot at making a real relationship work. With each passing second, he was more and more certain.

She snuggled against his chest, and he stroked her silky hair. He was going to have to come clean. She needed to know his father had the wrong idea about why Stuart was with her. She needed to know that he'd been pushed toward her in the first place to gain a business advantage. He cringed. It might be easier to sit on the ugly truth, but he couldn't risk that information getting back to her in some warped way. Absolutely not. His father and Ethan needed to know he wasn't playing any more games where Angie was concerned.

He cared about her way too much for that.

Her lips smoothed along the line of his jaw, and he knew he couldn't tell her right now. Not while they were still entwined, their breathing synced in perfect rhythm under the night sky.

He didn't want a single word to ruin this moment.

Chapter Eleven

A rattling coaxed coherent thoughts from Angie's brain. "Somebody's phone," she said. "Is that you or me?" Considering she'd seen him leave his in the car, it was a silly question.

She pushed off him, dropped her feet to the ground, and crouched on wobbly legs to retrieve her jeans. "Who would be calling me at midnight?"

Six months ago, she would've expected her mother on the other end with bad news about Nonna. But that call had come and gone … and she'd survived.

When the wind picked up, a chill blanketed her skin, making her suddenly conscious of her nakedness. She'd just had sex in an unfinished skyscraper with Stuart Perrault. There wasn't a way to top that, was there?

She yanked the phone from her pocket and saw Tony's smiling face on the screen.

"Shit. It's my brother." *This can't be good.* He never called in the middle of the night unless … "Hey." She was breathless.

"Trish is in labor."

"But she isn't due for three more months."

"I know. Ma's watching Angelina, but I wanted you to know."

Because he needs me. "Are you at Magee? I'll be there as soon as I can."

When she turned around after scrambling into her jeans, Stuart was pulling on his clothes. "Is something wrong with Trish?"

That shouldn't hurt like it did. He was being kind … caring, like a gentleman should be. "She's in labor. I need you to take me home. I have to go to the hospital."

"Of course. I hope everything is okay."

Again, she flinched. The unmistakable concern in his voice made her wonder. Was he still in love with Trish?

"I'll call you at some point with an update."

How fast could she get to the bottom of this building? She needed to get out of here. Cool down. Get her head on what she could really trust. What was really important. Her family.

"Thank you for tonight." He grabbed her hand and smoothed his thumb over her knuckles. One tiny tug and she stumbled against him.

Her thoughts from a moment ago seemed silly. "Thank you," she said, placing a gentle kiss on his soft lips. "I hope we get to do it again."

"Definitely."

But as she pulled into the hospital parking garage, the second thoughts piled on. Sex with Stuart Perrault was probably the stupidest thing she'd ever done. She still couldn't be sure he wasn't using her like some pawn in a life-sized chess match with his brother. And the city hadn't agreed to sell those properties to her yet. She and Stuart could be right back at each other's throats—and not in a good way—tomorrow. Besides, if she kept this up, Tony was going to find out sooner or later. God, she couldn't even consider that now. Now was not the time to be fretting about her sudden and unexpected sex life with the man who'd once had a sex life with her best friend.

By the time she walked into Trish's room, she'd pushed thoughts of Stuart from her head—almost. Little flickers of the night they shared remained, especially when her clothes brushed against the tender skin on her back and ass. Cement walls were not a giving surface. And her inner thighs. Man, they ached.

"Hey." Tony looked white as a ghost, which was saying something for a first generation Italian-American. He hovered over Trish, who was attached to a half dozen different machines. If their faces didn't give away the severity of the situation, the miles of wires and constant beeping sure did.

"What's going on?" she asked.

Trish opened her mouth, but only managed a squeak, and then tears rolled down her cheeks.

Tony kissed his wife's forehead and smoothed her hair. "It's okay, babe. Everything's going to be okay."

Angie grabbed onto Trish's IV-free hand and squeezed. "Is it full-blown labor?"

Trish nodded. "I'm one centimeter dilated and super thin." The fear in her voice had Angie bracing for the worst.

"So what happens next?"

"They got her pumped full of antibiotics and magnesium to stop the contractions," Tony said.

"And steroid shots," Trish said in between sniffles.

"For the baby's lungs," Tony said. "In case they can't get this under control and he makes an early entrance."

Crap. She tried her damnedest to stay positive. "So he's going to be a risk taker, just like his dad."

At least that made Tony smile.

"I can't believe this is happening," Trish said. "I did everything I was supposed to do. I followed the same routine I did when I was pregnant with Angelina. I don't understand."

"*Shh.*" Tony kissed her again. "Don't get worked up, babe. Things happen. You're in the best place now. They'll make sure everything is okay."

Gah! Angie felt helpless. "What can I do? I want to do something. Do you need anything from home? Nightgown? Slippers? Tone, do you need a coffee? A newspaper? Tell me what to do." She'd never been the kind of person to sit around when her family was in need.

Trish squeezed her hand. "You can't do anything right now, but it sure would take a load off my mind if you could be at

Worthington's tomorrow afternoon when the wallpaper goes in. Lydia is still too tentative around work crews to manage a project on her own. They walk all over her. I thought I had three more months to train her and help her build a backbone, but it looks like I don't. You can handle it. I know you can. You know my expectations well enough to be my eyes and ears and make sure the job is done right."

"Don't worry about work," Tony said.

"I have to worry about work. There's a schedule to keep and crews to be paid and clients who would like to move back into their homes."

"I'll be there." She didn't know how she'd fit it all in considering her crew was set to start a new flip in the South Side tomorrow, and they still had carpentry work at Trish's other active projects. But she'd be wherever her family needed her to be.

"Thank you."

Tony echoed Trish's gratitude, and for a second Angie wanted to yell, "Who's going to run my business while I'm running Trish's business? What the hell is wrong with you that you don't worry about the company our father started?" But the impulse faded. Now was not the time to open old wounds anyway. Besides, her brother had a wife and an unborn son to worry about, and he had a little girl at home. That was enough responsibility for one person.

She would be fine on her own. She'd been flying solo for a while now.

A few hours later, Trish calmed enough to fall asleep. Tony walked down the hall to call Ma and check on Angelina, and Angie wandered outside the room for a break from the mind-numbing beeping.

Now, she could read the text from Stuart.

Couldn't sleep. Keep thinking of you. Hope everything is okay. If you need anything, call. I'll hold your ladder.

She slumped against the wall as a weird combination of desire and relief poured over her. Every part of her wanted that man—even the parts that were still aching from having him already.

She'd trusted him tonight. She wanted to trust him going forward. But was it smart?

"Hey."

She jumped at the sound of Tony's voice.

"Trish's mom and dad will be here soon," he said. "When they get here, I'm gonna run home and see Angelina for a bit. You should go, too. Get some rest." He grabbed her shoulder and squeezed.

She winced. He'd hit the rawest spot on her shoulder.

"You okay?"

"I'm fine. Just a little sore."

"Work?"

Well, there was a cement wall, a flight of stairs, and lots of sweat. She guessed she could call it work. "Yep."

"All the more reason you should go home and get some sleep. Thank you for being here."

"Anytime." Every time. She had Tony's ladder. Always did. Things would be so much easier if he had hers.

Maybe then Stuart Perrault wouldn't be so tempting.

•••

Angie called the hospital on the way to the South Side and her latest flip. Trish was still being aggressively monitored, but they were cautiously optimistic since the contractions had been MIA for the last few days.

"I'll swing by later tonight and give you an update on the wallpaper." Which should thankfully be completed today, putting some wiggle room back into Angie's schedule.

"Take pictures," Trish said.

"Okay." If she remembered. She had a lot on her mind.

Still no word from the city about her offer on the row homes. And this past week of juggling her work and Trish's had her bone tired—and missing Stuart.

Her yawn turned into a smile when she thought about him. "Trish?" *I slept with Stuart.* But she caught herself. What if that upset Trish? What if that made things worse for her and the baby? "Take care of yourself," she said instead.

"I have no choice. There are a dozen doctors and nurses checking on me day and night, and their hovering is nothing compared to your brother's. I adore that man, but he can be so intense."

Angie chuckled. She was definitely going to tell Trish about Stuart, just not today and not over the phone.

Ten minutes later, she parked in front of the narrow two-story she was hoping would net her a considerable profit.

"Morning, Ange."

She nodded in Dante's direction.

"Did you notice I didn't say good?"

Shit. "What happened?"

"We opened up those walls upstairs and found active knob and tube."

So much for the updated wiring she'd been so happy to see in the basement. "They only converted half the house."

"Yep. Because it was easy to do the first floor with an unfinished basement. The second floor with a finished attic space, not so much. I called Matt in to take a look."

She winced at the mention of her friend and electrician, knowing he was already cutting her a break on the existing electrical work. This was going to cost her.

"Ange, can you come look at this?" A voice rose up through the floorboards.

"Now what?" With a sigh, she headed to the basement where a few of her guys were putting in a French drain under the guidance of Trish's plumbing guru, Krebs.

Hiccups in the flip were not what she needed on a day when she was supposed to cut out early to finish up a kitchen project in South Fayette and then eyeball the finished wallpaper at the Worthington house in Fox Chapel.

"What's up?" she called out when she hit the bottom step.

A gaping hole filled the back half of the basement.

"Your water issue has less to do with rain and more to do with pipes that weren't properly connected," Krebs said. "Look at this."

She didn't want to. She knew all she would see was more dollar signs.

Her phone rang, and she recognized the exchange of City Hall. Had they made a decision about her offer? She shushed the guys in the basement and turned her back on them.

"Hello?"

"Angie? It's Jana Wright from the building office."

"Yes?"

"Sorry it's taken so long to hear from us, and unfortunately, I don't have a final decision, yet. I did, however, want to call and let you know that under these special circumstances, we've decided to announce a formal bid period in case other investors would be interested in purchasing and moving the houses. It's not that we've disregarded your offer; it's just that multiple offers will ensure a sale is guaranteed should the chosen bid fall through for some reason. Having a pool of back-ups to pick from would prevent further delays of the highway project. We hope you understand. We will close the formal bid period in two weeks, and then contact all interested parties with our final decision."

Great. More waiting … and the potential for competition. Although, at this very moment, with knob and tube wiring and inefficient plumbing draining her budget dry, she wasn't all that excited about going into debt to save any more derelict houses.

By the time five o'clock rolled around, she was just finishing up at the kitchen renovation, and she was tired, sore, and in no mood to drive across town to put her stamp of approval on some wallpaper. Still, she climbed into her truck and made her way to Fox Chapel, bitching her way through traffic on 28, because she'd promised Trish she would.

Lydia met her on the sprawling front porch. "It looks good. I hope you think it looks good. There are a couple corners that bubble the smallest bit, but I couldn't decide if it was a real problem or if I was being neurotic. I asked the guys for their opinion, but they looked at me like I was an idiot."

Probably because Lydia was five feet tall on a good day and dressed in comic-book-inspired clothes she'd made by hand. A ginger-headed pixie doused in geek dust was a little hard to take seriously.

"I'm sure it's fine," Angie said, stifling a yawn with the back of her hand. "Show me the bubbles."

"There," Lydia said as she stepped into the foyer and pointed to the upper right corner.

The purple and silver pattern was so damn busy Angie's vision blurred. "I don't see any bubbles."

"Oh, thank God. When I asked what would happen if they needed to come out and fix anything, he said it would have to be next week at the earliest. I knew that wouldn't fly with Trish. She's a stickler for her budget and her schedule. Which would mean I'd have to be forceful and get them out here sooner. I'm not really good at forceful."

So Angie would be tapped to take care of that, too. "Well, it looks good to me." Thank God, because she didn't have any more time to devote on this place.

While Lydia wandered around the house, turning off lights and locking up doors, Angie snapped pictures of the finished project for Trish and dreamed of taking a long hot shower and crawling into bed.

A hissing sounded from the first floor powder room, followed by Lydia's screams.

What the … ? She raced down the main hall. "What happened?"

Lydia was drenched. "I don't know! I just sat down to pee."

Water spewed from behind the toilet, arching over the bowl and splattering over the seat and floor like the fountain in Point State Park.

Angie dove for the shut off valve.

"The hardwoods! What are we going to do?"

"Find something to soak up this water."

Lydia returned with a drop cloth the painters left behind. "I don't know if it's absorbent."

It wasn't, but they did the best they could. Then, Lydia remembered a beach towel she'd stashed in a bag in her trunk. That saved the floor. God only knew what was going on with the plumbing.

Angie dialed Tony's number as she made her way through the empty house to the basement to do some detective work.

"Hey," he answered.

"Hey, listen, I didn't want to upset Trish, so I'm calling you first to see how she's doing."

"Hang on." There was rustling on the other end, and then his faint words, "Babe, I'm going to take this one in the hall. I'll be right back."

She hit the bottom basement step, and sure enough, water ran along the first-floor joists and puddled on the cement floor.

"Okay, what's the problem?" Tony asked.

Main shut off valve, she thought. Where the hell was it?

"We have a plumbing issue," she said.

"Where?"

"At the Fox Chapel house."

"Shit."

She located the valve and turned it off. "I'll have Lydia call Krebs and get him over here as soon as possible. Just don't say anything to Trish until we have all the information. I'm going to forward you the pics of the wallpaper. It looks great. Show her that, and then tell her I can't make it to the hospital tonight because … I have a date."

Silence, and then he cleared his throat. "Do you have a date?"

"Yeah, with a plumber, jackass. Unless you plan on leaving your wife and taking care of this for me."

"I was planning on leaving here in a couple hours to relieve Ma and spend the night at home with Angelina. I could swing by."

"Don't bother." The fact that he offered was nice. "I'm sure Ma needs the break, and your daughter wants to see you more than I do."

"Okay, but you call me if you need anything."

"You, too."

She made it as far as the top of the steps before her phone rang. *Stuart.* She smiled.

"Hey, hold that thought," she said as she answered his call, and then she held the phone against her shoulder and shouted to Lydia, "Get Krebs on the line and get him out here ASAP."

With the phone back to her ear, she walked toward the front door. "Hi."

"That didn't sound good. Why do you need a plumber?"

"We've got a toilet that thinks he's a geyser over at one of Trish's remodels."

"You're there now?"

"Yep."

"So my chances of dragging you away and taking you to dinner are slim to none?"

"Sorry, looks like you'll be eating at the counter tonight." And she and Lydia would probably be ordering pizza to be delivered here.

He chuckled. "It doesn't have to be dinner. How about dessert? Or a beer? I just want to see you again. Soon. Maybe you could stop by on your way home?"

"Churchill is not on my way home."

"Small technicality." She could hear the smile in his voice.

Sitting on the top step, she rested her back against the bannister and stretched her legs across the wood slats. It was the closest she'd been to relaxed all day. "I'll see what I can do. I'd like to see you, too."

"I could always come to you."

Boy, that was a nice thought, and she almost agreed. But, the idea of inviting him to one of Trish's projects, where she would have to explain to Lydia exactly who he was and why he was there, wasn't appealing. "God no. I wouldn't wish this crap on anyone."

"You sound tired."

"I am. Long day. Lots of unforeseen drama. Jana Wright called to say they're going to accept offers from interested investors for the next two weeks."

"Yeah, I heard that from Simon, too, but there are no new offers, and he doesn't expect any. It's not like they are advertising this. They just don't want to get blamed for mishandling anything else as far as this project is concerned. You have nothing to worry about."

She was too tired to worry anyway.

The screen door opened behind her. "Krebs is on the phone. He wants to talk to you."

She held up a finger. "One second. I'll be right in."

"Go ahead," Stuart said. "We can talk about this later … in person … when you stop by on your way home."

Despite the crap day she'd had, she was smiling.

He had that effect on her.

• • •

Stuart flipped on the outside light, illuminating his front porch, and opened the door. Churchill might not be on Angie's way home, but she'd found her way here all the same. At nearly ten o'clock, he'd almost given up on her.

"Hey," he said as she hopped out of the truck.

"Hey." Her shoulders rounded forward, and she shuffled her feet as she walked up his front steps. "It's so late. I probably shouldn't have come."

"Nonsense. I'm glad you're here." He pulled her into his arms and smoothed her hair, feeling her warm body go limp against his.

The need to take care of her overwhelmed him.

He led her inside to the living room, where he sat in an oversized chair and pulled her onto his lap. "Relax."

She pushed against his chest. "I'm going to get your pajamas dirty with my work clothes."

"I don't care. They're just sweatpants. And this is just a T-shirt." He pinched the fabric and pulled it away from his chest. "I don't sleep in either."

She raised her brows and grinned. "What do you sleep in?"

"Why don't you stay long enough to find out?"

She stared at him, the grin fading into a small smile, and then she rested her head on his shoulder and flattened a hand over his heart.

Could she feel how hard it was beating? He was crazy for her.

"Did you get the plumbing mess fixed?" he asked.

"Which one?"

"I didn't realize you had more than one issue."

"I have two." She traced a circular pattern over his bicep, littering his skin with tiny bumps and hardening his nipples. "Improperly connected pipes in my South Side flip and a manufacturer's defect in a toilet in Fox Chapel. I also have knob and tube wiring on the second floor of the flip, and the wrong base cabinets for a South Fayette kitchen renovation. And no end to the ridiculous hours I've been working in sight, because my sister-in-law is still in the hospital, and … crap! I sound like an awful person, don't I? It's not like she can help being in the hospital."

He nodded and smoothed a hand over her back. "How is she? Any update?"

"So far so good. Labor seems to have stalled."

Sometimes it still felt so odd to be hearing about Trish in such a detached way. He'd been with her for two years. They'd discussed marriage and family. It was one of the reasons he'd though they were a perfect match. Their personalities aligned as well as their family values and backgrounds did. It could've been him by her side at the hospital instead of Tony.

So strange.

But holding Angie in his arms, resting his cheek against the top of her head, he was little more than marginally concerned for Trish, and he lacked his usual unfavorable reaction to anything having to do with Tony.

"How's your brother holding up?"

She looked at him, surprise sparkling in her eyes. "Um … he's okay. Worried."

"I bet. His wife and unborn child are in the hospital, and there's nothing he can do to help them. That has to be a man's worst fear." God knew it would be his if he had a wife and child to worry about.

He reflexively brushed his lips across the top of her head and squeezed her tighter. The minute he did it, he felt stupid. No matter how much he wanted to make a go of this, they weren't exactly on the fast track toward commitment and family. Hell, he couldn't even get up enough nerve to tell her everything he wanted to tell her.

Angie snuggled in again, head to his chest, and he traced a finger along the bump of her wrist. Before he knew it, he was smiling again.

"Enough about them," he said. "How are you?"

"Aside from tired, I'm overwhelmed … with everything." She sat up. "And I really shouldn't be here. I have to be onsite at the flip by seven tomorrow morning in order to get to South Fayette in time for the replacement cabinets to be delivered. I haven't been sleeping as it is. I desperately need a shower."

Smoothing a hand against her cheek, he pressed his thumb against her lips. "I have a bed … and a shower. You're welcome to both."

She didn't protest when he led her to his slate-lined steam shower, and with the push of a button he filled the glass enclosure with curls of steam.

"Towels are here." He pointed to a huge, lidded basket beside him. "Soap, shampoo, and the like are on the ledge. When you're finished, you can wrap up in this." He grabbed his gray robe off a hook by the door and laid it on the bench beside the glass shower door.

She nodded, but she didn't move.

Did she want him to join her? No, he couldn't. Not that he didn't want to. But she was tired and overwhelmed. She didn't need him draining whatever she had left.

"Why are you looking at me like that?" he asked.

A beautiful grin tipped the corners of her lips. "It's an awfully big shower for one person."

He chuckled. "I just spent the last fifteen seconds telling myself you didn't need me in that shower with you. You're exhausted. It seems very slimy for me to make a move on you when you're feeling like that."

"Most guys would."

The guys she'd told him about anyway. And that didn't sit right with him.

"I'm not most guys," he said.

Her bottom lip pushed out and the corners of her eyes drooped. "Don't pout. It makes me feel like I'm doing something wrong."

"You're not."

"I know."

And yet she unbuttoned her jeans without taking her sparking eyes off of him.

He couldn't help it—he watched her fingers work. His breath hitched as she pushed the denim and her panties into a puddle on the floor.

When he looked her in the eyes again, she smiled. "You're a really good man, Stuart—a decent man." Then, she pulled her shirt over her head and removed her bra.

Two full, pert breasts made his mouth water.

He groaned, but somehow managed to smile. "And you're a very bad woman."

"I try," she said, stepping toward him and then lifting his T-shirt over his stomach. Her warm hands flattened over his abs, stirring his desire. "You should clean me up a bit, wash away the filth."

When she tossed his shirt aside, he kissed her, long and slow, hoping it would be enough to satisfy him. Then, before he lost his mind and she pushed him too far, he broke away, reached behind her to open the glass door, and turned the steam to a steady stream of hot water.

"Get in the shower," he growled.

She stepped in, and a moan of pleasure left her lips.

Leaving this room, knowing she was in here, looking and sounding like that, was torture.

"This is amazing," she said. "You should really be in here with me."

Damn it. He had his sweatpants off before he took his next breath.

Chapter Twelve

Stuart stared at an ugly purple and yellow bruise on Angie's shoulder blade. He grazed the spot, and her muscles twitched. "How'd you do this?"

"Well, some guy thought it was a good idea to have sex against a cement wall." She turned her head slightly, and he could see she was smiling.

But he wasn't.

He'd hurt her. He didn't want that. He stepped closer and brushed his lips against the spot. He had never wanted to hurt her. Things had just heated up so fast.

Slipping his hands beneath her arms, he skimmed the curves of her waist and hips. She made him want like he'd never wanted before, but he needed to be careful with that. It was time to slow down. Back off. Prove to her he wasn't a jerk like the other guys who'd used her and left her damaged.

She braced her hands on the wall and spread her feet apart, readying for whatever she expected him to deliver. He could definitely give it. His erect penis ached as it grazed the small of her back. But he bit the side of his cheek and turned away, grabbing a bottle of shampoo off the stone ledge.

"Step out of the water for a minute."

When she turned and saw his hands full of liquid soap, she smiled. "Lubrication."

He bit his cheek again. "I'm going to wash your hair."

Her eyes widened. "Seriously?"

He nodded, and she stepped back into the stream of water, thoroughly wetting her head. Droplets rode the curves of her neck and breasts to drip off her hardened nipples. It was so damned erotic. If he were less of a man, he'd have begged her to touch him and put him out of his misery. Instead, he pulled her from the water and ran his soapy hands through her hair.

Her eyes were open at first. Her lashes clumped together. But as he pressed his fingertips into tiny circles over her scalp, they fluttered and closed, and then she moaned.

That sound. It ripped through him leaving the most intense ache behind.

One kiss. He slipped his slippery hands to her neck and pressed his lips to hers. "Feel good?"

"Heavenly." She moaned again when he dropped his hands lower over her chest to her swollen breasts.

"Good." So good.

He dumped more soap into his hand and smoothed his palms along the curves of her ass, between her legs, lingering longer than he had to. Back and forth over the hard nub.

Her moans escalated.

When she came at him with open mouth, he leaned away. "No. Just relax. Don't worry about me."

She opened one eye and smirked. "Why the martyr routine?"

"I like the view."

Her breath hitched when he leaned forward to suck a drop of water from her nipple.

"No way," she managed, despite his fingers working her toward orgasm. "You feel bad about my back, don't you? This is your apology."

"Maybe."

"It's …" she dug her fingernails into his shoulder and lifted a wet leg to his hip, opening wider for him, "not a big deal."

"I hurt you. I don't like to hurt people."

She tossed her head back and screamed out as she bucked against him.

"I'd much rather make you feel like that." He kissed her neck, and then stepped back. "Now, rinse."

As much as he ached to give himself the same release, he raised his hands to neutral territory again, gently cupping her shoulders and guiding her back into the stream.

When she was suds free, he reached behind her to stop the water flow, and then wrapped her wet hair in a towel and dried her beautiful body right down to her surprisingly pink painted toes.

By the time he was done, the insides of his cheeks were raw from all the biting meant to keep his libido in check, but his softening erection seemed to have gotten the message.

"You're too good to be true," she said, adding a sigh.

"No. I'm not." He took her by the hand and led her to his bed.

"And now I suppose you want me to sleep. For real."

"Exactly."

She grinned. "Killjoy."

He pulled back the covers and watched her slide against the sheets, but not before she disrobed. His self-control was getting one hell of a workout tonight.

Back on his side, he crawled into bed and faced her. The hair he'd washed was still wrapped in a towel, and the absence of those inky strands made her olive skin and espresso-colored eyes seem brighter. She looked good. In here. With him.

"Thank you," she said.

He smoothed a hand against her cheek. "You're welcome."

"But I can't sleep in. I have to be onsite at seven. I have to get home and change my clothes."

"I know." He rolled over to face his nightstand and adjust his alarm clock.

When he rolled back again, her eyes were closed, and her breathing was even.

Eventually, he dozed off, too, and when he woke like clockwork at five, he carried her clothes to the laundry room, hoping to buy her another hour of sleep. While they washed, he showered and shaved. While they dried, he dressed, checked emails, and then decided to make eggs. But he was sidetracked when his phone rang.

It was his father. Before he even got to the office.

This ought to be good. "Hello."

"Pull her off."

"Excuse me?"

"The Corcarelli girl. Pull her off the row houses. I had drinks with Louie Carmichael last night, and he wants those houses. I talked to the mayor this morning, and he confirmed they were open to other offers. He also made it clear he wants to keep everything as cordial as possible between all parties involved going forward, which means he doesn't want a fight. Pull her off, so Louie can secure the row homes peacefully."

Stuart didn't want a fight either, and he didn't see the need to fight now. "Why not pull Louie off?"

His father laughed. "Son, Louie is bidding on the old Watergate Hotel. If he gets that project off the ground, I want to be a part of it. That boy is going places. You need to learn to recognize the train worth hitching up to. Fortunately, Ethan seems to have that part down."

Of course he does.

"So pull her off," his father continued. "I don't care how you do it. Just convince her to withdraw her name from the list of prospective buyers. It shouldn't be hard. I saw the way she looks at you. And just think, you'll be doing her a favor. She's small potatoes. We both know it's a stretch for her to afford an undertaking like this."

Angie stepped into the kitchen, wrapped in his robe. Her hair fell in chunky waves around her face. He couldn't play with her emotions and hurt her like that.

"I have to go," he said, and then he disconnected the call before his father could speak again. He was going to hear about the brushoff at the office.

But he wasn't at the office yet.

"Hey." He crossed to her, wrapped his arms around her waist, and buried his face in her warm neck. "Did you sleep well?"

"I did. I like your bed. I would've liked a few more hours in it."

"I bet." He would've liked a few more hours of peace instead of his father's phone call. "Coffee?" He reluctantly let her go and grabbed the nearest mug, filling it up and passing it off to her. "I was going to make eggs."

"This is enough." She took a good long sip, letting the mug linger at her lips. All the while her dark eyes sparkled at him from over the rim.

He snapped his fingers. "Clothes. I washed them. They're in the dryer." He started to move past her. "Let me …"

But she caught him by the necktie. "Why the rush?"

"I don't want you to be late."

She glanced at the wall clock. "Well, now that you washed my clothes, I don't have to stop home. I can spare a few minutes."

Leaning into him, she reached behind him and set the coffee mug on the counter. "Come back to bed." She smiled. "There will be no martyrs today, Perrault."

She dragged him back to the bedroom by the necktie.

• • •

The next week flew by. Before Angie knew it, Friday rolled around again. As she stepped out of her filthy work clothes and made her way to the shower, she caught a glimpse of her neglected Popsicle stick house. It'd been a few weeks since she'd worked on it. The last time was with Stuart.

She smiled into the stinging spray of hot water. Too bad he wasn't here to help her with it now … or with this shower … or earlier today when they'd discovered cracks in the foundation of the South Side flip. Cracks her friend who'd acted as inspector had missed. Those types of structural things were a little over her head, but they'd be basic to Stuart.

She'd ask his opinion tonight over dinner, since she'd been unable to get ahold of him during the day. His work must've been hammering him like her work had been hammering her. They both needed a little downtime.

Unfortunately, she got called to Tony's house forty-five minutes before Stuart was supposed to pick her up for dinner.

Rushing into the impeccably decorated Victorian, she found a pale Aunt Connie raising her arm overhead with a wad of paper towels wrapped around her hand.

"Go get that taken care of," Angie said, as she reached toward her mother to grab a sniveling Angelina.

"Honey, thank you so much for coming," her mother said. 'I'll get Aunt Connie to urgent care, and then we'll be back. You look so nice. You were going someplace special, weren't you?"

"Just dinner. It's no big deal. Nothing like almost cutting off your finger." She looked at Aunt Connie. "Please go. Now."

When they were gone, she settled onto the couch in the family room with her niece and read a few books. And when the little girl got caught up in some singing and dancing television show, she called Stuart.

"I'm sorry."

"I understand," he said.

"I wanted to see you."

"I wanted to see you, too. Later."

"I don't know how long this will take. You know the emergency room. And it's not life threatening, so they'll sit there forever. Trish is being moved to the pre-term labor side of the unit, and Tony won't leave until she's settled. It'll be too late for dinner for sure."

"Dinner was just an excuse to see you in a dress. As long as that still happens, I won't complain."

She smiled and ran a hand down Angelina's back as the child's eyes closed.

A half hour later, Angelina was still asleep, and Angie kicked off her heels and roamed the big house, looking at the black-and-white family photos Trish had filling every room. Vin and Tony helping Nonna make pizelles, their arms elbow deep in mixing bowls, while Nonna grinned. She needed a copy of that photo. And this one. Her father and mother holding baby Tony in a frilly-ass christening gown. *Ha!* He had to hate that picture. Or maybe not. Fatherhood had changed him. Hell, Trish had changed him.

A shadow in the shape of a person on the front porch caught her eye. Maybe he was home early. Maybe she could make it to dinner after all.

She opened the front door to find Stuart holding a large, brown paper bag.

"Delivery," he said with a smile. And then he took in her little black dress. "Damn. You look hot."

For a minute, all that mattered was the sexy sparkle in his eyes, but then she remembered where they were. "Are you crazy? What if Tony comes home?"

"You said he wouldn't be home until late. I figured we could eat, and I could run before he got here."

"What about Angelina? If she wakes up, she'll tell everyone you were here."

"She doesn't know who I am. Besides, if she wakes up, I'll hide. She's three. How hard can it be to pull one over on a toddler?"

Angie shook her head, but she grinned. "I feel like I'm a teenage babysitter sneaking a guy into the house after I put the kids to bed."

"Did you do that?"

"All the time."

"Then you have experience." He winked. "We'll be fine."

Once he was inside and the door was closed, he wrapped an arm around her waist and pulled her in for a kiss. Sweet at first, but then mouths opened and desire exploded, and before she knew it her back was against the door and the hem of her dress was ringing her waist.

In Tony and Trish's house with Angelina sleeping in the other room.

"Not here." She held his face in her hands. Their heavy breathing echoed in the silence.

He dropped his forehead to hers and smoothed her dress into place. "You're probably right."

"I wish I weren't."

He chuckled and picked the paper bag off the floor where he'd dropped it.

She led him to the dining room, and then she looked in on Angelina, who was still zonked. A warm, fuzzy feeling swelled in her chest. She loved her niece … but she loved her fifteen minutes ago, too, and she hadn't felt like this.

It wasn't about Angelina, was it?

Stuart was waiting for her in the dining room. Was this what it would feel like to have a family of her own with a man she couldn't keep her hands off of? Like what Tony and Trish had found in each other. The gag-inducing googly eyes and not-so-secret make-out sessions in Ma's pantry suddenly made sense.

But she was getting ahead of herself, wasn't she? A life like that was built on more than a few weeks of really great sex.

She walked into the dining room and saw a small box of brick oven pizza, two bottles of beer, a container of salad, and a lighted candle. *Pizza and beer.* He was good to her. Too good, maybe?

She ignored the doubt.

He pulled out a chair. "Dinner is served." His words were hushed, and for some reason that prompted years of future, stolen moments like this to flash before her eyes.

"Thank you." The words caught in her throat.

She was crazy to want this, wasn't she? To want him?

"Onions and green pepper," he said as he served her a slice. "I hope I got that right."

"Perfect. It smells amazing."

"Good." He kissed her cheek, and then sat across from her.

They slipped effortlessly into conversation about her workweek, Trish's health status, and Aunt Connie's finger injury.

Before she knew it, her beer was empty, and her belly was full.

"What about you?" she asked. "How's work?"

He sat back in his chair, folded his arms over his chest, and looked away. "Same old, same old. But, there's progress with the Build Together Pittsburgh Kids idea." He looked at her again, and smiled. "We may be able to expand it beyond neighborhood rec centers. I talked to the superintendent, and he's very interested in bringing the program into the city schools."

"That's awesome."

"And you're going to help me, right?"

She wanted to. But how could she add anything else to her schedule?

"Daddy!" Angelina called.

Angie's heart rocketed into her throat, and she jumped out of her chair. Tony was here?

"She's up," Stuart said, and he moved into the darkened living room.

She's up. That's all. Angie opened her mouth for bigger breaths. "Coming, baby."

Angelina sat on the couch, rubbing her eyes. "I want Daddy."

"He'll be home soon." But not before Stuart leaves. *Please, God.*

Hopefully Stuart was cleaning up and plotting his escape right now.

She scooped her niece up and held her close.

In the distance, the front door opened and closed, and she relaxed against the overstuffed arm of the couch. She'd call him later … or maybe stop by on her way home. Even though Churchill wasn't on her way home. She smiled into Angelina's strawberry-scented hair.

"Ange?"

Fuck! That was Tony's voice.

"You here?" he asked.

"Daddy!" Angelina slid from her lap and sprinted out of the family room.

Angie was right behind her.

Oh my God. Oh my God. Oh my God. Where was Stuart? How was she going to explain this?

"You're home early," she said, her eyes flashing to the dining room where proof of her dinner remained.

Tony whistled as he lifted his little one into his arms. "And Ma was right. She called to see if I could get home sooner rather than later. Said you were dressed up. You are. What gives?"

Her face was on fire. Her eyes wouldn't stop focusing on the dining room door. *Was Stuart still here?* "I, uh, had dinner plans."

He glanced over his shoulder. "Why the hell do you keep looking …?"

"Who's that man?" Angelina asked. She pointed down the hallway that led to the front door.

"Tony, don't freak out." Angie dashed into the hall to run interference between the two men.

"Evening," Stuart said.

Thank God for Angelina, because Tony opened his mouth, looked at his little girl, and then he closed it again. But his wide, crazy eyes made things loud and clear.

"I had dinner plans with Stuart, and then Aunt Connie got hurt, so he brought dinner here to me."

She didn't think it possible, but Tony's eyes grew wider. "A business dinner? Dressed like that?"

God, he looked like her dad. "Not exactly."

"Leave," he said.

She wasn't sure whom he was talking to, probably both of them. "Okay."

"Don't be mad at her," Stuart said. "It was my fault. I just showed up."

"You just showed up?" Tony's voice grew louder. "It's like freaking déjà vu. Remember the last time you just showed up at this door? I should've decked you like I'd wanted to. Then maybe you wouldn't be here now, sniffing around my sister who's dressed like that."

"Oh, for crying out loud, Tony! Don't even. I'm a grown woman, and there is nothing wrong with this dress or my choice of dinner date." She looked at Angelina and smiled. "It's a pretty dress. Right, princess?" Little ears. Little eyes. She hoped Tony would take the hint.

"It's different, now," Stuart said. "The last time I was here was a mistake. I didn't know she was with you. I never would've come had I known you were here."

"Yeah, so what's your excuse now? You had to know there was a damn good chance I'd show up again. It's *my* house."

"Angie was here, and she's worth the risk."

She looked at him. He stood strong at the end of the hall, dressed in black, with his hands in his pockets like an outlaw at thirty paces. And she wanted him. Bad.

Stuart was worth the risk, too.

"We'll talk about this later," she said to Tony, and then she kissed Angelina's cheek. "Night, princess. I have to go."

"You're going to leave with him?" Tony asked.

"You bet I am." Normally what her family wanted and needed came first, but not this time. "I got used to you and Trish being together, Tone. You'll get used to this."

Because *this* was worth fighting for.

Chapter Thirteen

Ethan kicked his feet out in front of him and lounged in the chair at the end of Stuart's dining table. "Listen, I know we left things kind of rough between us the other day, but I'm starting to get a little worried about you."

Thank God Angie had left a few hours before his brother had barged in on what had started out as the perfect Saturday.

Stuart rolled his eyes. "I bet you are."

"Come on, man. I'm not the enemy. At least, I don't want to be. What is going on with you? Why haven't you been at work?"

"I just wanted some time off."

"A week?" Ethan shook his head. "I don't know if I can buy that, especially not after our argument. Something else is going on. I have to agree with Dad. The timing is suspicious. He asked you to pull Angie off the houses, and you haven't been back to work since."

"Well, there's something new—you agreeing with Dad."

"Can we talk about this without it becoming an us-against-you thing?"

He sighed. "I don't know. Can we?" It had been like that for such a long time.

Ethan unleashed his charismatic grin. "Let's give it a shot."

"Fine. It's more than a vacation." He roughed a hand over his face. "I need some space. You were sort of right. It's not that I don't care. It's just that I'm not altogether happy at The Perrault Group." There. He'd said it. He'd been thinking about it for a while now. Ever since his driveway confrontation with Ethan, really. Unless he was at the BTP offices or with Angie, he was miserable.

Ethan nodded. "Okay. Admitting you have a problem is the first step toward conquering it." He flashed a quick grin, but then his brow creased. "What I can't figure out is why you're so unhappy, man. Are you still stewing about Paris, or is it something else?" Ethan scratched his head. "I mean, you give me a lot of guff about my relationship with dad. Is that it? You're jealous? Because you could have golfed with us or had drinks with us. You were always invited. You just chose not to come."

All true. He was jealous, but he didn't want to admit it. In fact, part of him wanted to pick a fight again, because arguing with Ethan was much easier than admitting his own flaws. "Maybe. But the way I feel and the way I'm being treated is nothing compared to the way other people are being mistreated."

Ethan shook his head, his brow scrunched. "I'm not following."

"The people in that neighborhood who were never given a choice as to whether they wanted a highway running through it are being mistreated, and neither you nor Dad seems to care about that."

And Angie was being mistreated, too. His father and brother wanted to use her as some sort of bait to halt the lawsuit while Louie Carmichael walked away with the prize.

No way. Not if he could help it.

Ethan laughed. "Wow. I did not see that one coming. You start one nonprofit, and then you tumble off the socially conscious deep end. No wonder you're unhappy. They've got you feeling guilty about everything you've earned. Don't tell me you traded in the Beemer for a Prius."

"Don't be an ass. Those people don't have me feeling anything but sympathy for them and the way their wants and needs have been disregarded. This project has made me realize that there are more important things in life than money and progress, especially if people are getting hurt in the pursuit."

Ethan said nothing, simply sized him up with shrewd eyes for a moment. "Mmm. This project, huh? And what about Angie?"

He clenched his jaw. "What about her?"

"You're telling me she didn't have a part in this big revelation? C'mon, bro. Where do things stand with her?"

He wasn't about to get into his personal life with Ethan. "I won't ask her to back down from those row houses."

"Because you want to stick it to me and Louie, or because you're sleeping with her?" He grinned. "Oh, close your mouth, and don't try to deny it. Dad told me he caught you two in a *compromising position.*" Ethan bobbed his eyebrows. "Believe me. I don't blame you for hitting that. If the tables were turned, I would have. And you know the best part about it? It's all Dad's fault. He thought he was so smart pushing you to charm her in the first place. He just didn't count on her charming you and putting a wrench in his plan." He laughed so hard tears shone in the corners of his eyes.

Idiot. This wasn't a joke. "Leave Angie out of this."

Ethan shrugged. "Okay. Then *get* her out of this."

Stuart leaned forward, crossing his arms tightly over his chest. "Or what? Huh? If she doesn't back out, and she gets the houses, what's the worst that can happen? The highway project moves forward … and Louie crawls back into whatever hole he came from. To borrow a favorite phrase from Dad, everybody wins."

"There's your problem, bro. You're not looking at the big picture. If Louie loses, he could hold a grudge against us and not consider us for the Watergate Hotel project. How is that a win for The Perrault Group?" He looked to Stuart expectantly. "I mean, maybe you're such a Dudley Do-Gooder now that you don't care about the company, but I'm the one who brought Louie into this in the first place. If his offer doesn't get picked, it reflects poorly on me."

Opposite ends of the ring. Again.

Stuart frowned. "It doesn't have to be like this, you know? We could actually try to work together for once and figure this out."

"Hey, you're the one making this a competition. Like usual," his brother snorted. "'May the best man win.' That's what you said, right? Well, that's all I'm trying to do here."

"Jesus." His brother was right. Stuart rubbed his face in his hands. "We are the most dysfunctional family on the planet."

Ethan shook his head. "Nah, not even close. Remember the Jameses?"

The name triggered a vivid mental image of their childhood neighbors, mischievous redheaded twin brothers who had regularly wrestled naked on their impeccably landscaped lawn.

Stuart grimaced. "Oh God, thanks for that. I can still see that hand-slap shaped birthmark the shorter one had on his ass."

They both bust out laughing simultaneously, and for a blissful second, they were on the same side again.

But Ethan was right; it couldn't last. It never could. Especially not when they were after the same things. Stuart still had something to prove.

"I'm not going to try to convince Angie to back off," he said. She deserved those houses. And right now, whether he was proud of it or now, he wanted Ethan to feel the sting of defeat.

"Then you better be prepared to lose this project."

After the week he'd spent with Angie, it was easier to imagine losing the project than it was to imagine losing her.

• • •

Sunday dinner was going to be a nightmare.

Angie took a deep breath, and then checked her makeup in Stuart's bathroom mirror. Did she look different, like she'd been having regular sex? They were going to know something was up, weren't they? Her family had a nose for shit like this.

Face the music, Corcarelli. Or in this case, the inquisition. At least Tony wouldn't be at dinner. Nothing would get nasty. But he'd had plenty of time to tell everyone about what had happened two nights ago when he'd found her with Stuart.

"You look beautiful," Stuart said. He leaned against the doorjamb, a cup of coffee in one hand. How could he be so relaxed?

"I should've called Trish," she said. "She should've heard about us from me."

"I thought she already suspected something."

"She did. She does. But God only knows what Tony told her. He probably made it sound like we were having sex on their dining room table."

He crossed the room and pulled her against him. "Now, there's an idea."

"You need a bigger table, buddy."

"Consider it done. I have nothing else to do today." He nuzzled her neck and pulled her earlobe between his teeth.

Mmm. She was melting again. It was getting harder and harder to stay upright when he was around.

"You could come with me." *He could?* She straightened her head and gave it a little shake.

"You want me to come to your mother's house for Sunday dinner?"

"Well, you've already had dinner at my brother's house. Why not?"

He smiled. "You don't mean that."

"Sure, I do."

"Then why do you look scared to death that I'll agree to go?" He smacked a quick kiss to her lips. "You only offered because you felt sorry for me."

Was that why she'd asked? Maybe. But maybe not. Maybe she just wanted him there.

His home phone rang.

He glanced at his wristwatch, and wrinkles lined his face, but he didn't make a move to answer the call.

"Aren't you going to get that?" she asked.

"Nope. Probably telemarketers."

"Okay." She nodded as she backtracked to the conversation before the telephone interruption. "I don't feel sorry for you." She wrapped her arms around his neck and leaned into him, opening her mouth on his neck. "I'm just starting to get used to you being around. I like it. I like this."

"I'm not complaining." She heard his coffee cup hit the granite counter, and then felt his hands on her ass. "But we can't really do this in front of your family."

"Not in front of them, but my mother has a really big pantry."

He chuckled until her tongue rounded the curve of his Adam's apple. You could've heard a pin drop after that.

"Nobody but Tony bites," she said. "And he won't be there. Of course, I could bite … if you want me to."

His phone rang again.

"Damn it." He growled.

It seemed like an extreme reaction to telemarketers.

"Hold that thought." He left the room.

Angie stared at her reflection. Why did she feel like something bad was about to happen? She stepped into the bedroom, but she couldn't hear his voice, so she walked into the hallway, and then into den.

"I don't feel well. I've been sick all week. I don't care what Ethan told Dad. I just need a break. Mom, I'm fine. Yes, I'll see a doctor. I'll be at brunch next Sunday."

He was sick? He had been all week? He didn't look sick to her.

She scrambled back to the bedroom and tried to look innocent.

"You're not very sneaky," he said after he'd taken one look at her.

The pit in her stomach grew. "But you are. You were sick all week and you hid it from me."

"I'm … not sick."

"So, you're lying to your mother. Why?"

"It's not worth discussing."

"Why?" Yep. She raised her voice. She couldn't help it. Every part of her body was on high alert. "I want to know. I feel like it has something to do with me."

He shook his head. "Are you done in the bathroom?"

"Stuart! Look at me. Tell me what's going on."

"Angie, calm down. It's not a big deal."

She hated that. *Calm down, Angie. Take a pill. Relax. Chill.* She'd heard it said a million different ways over the years. "No! Tell me what's going on or I'm leaving."

"Fine." He sighed. "My father and I aren't seeing eye to eye on something."

"Something that has to do with me." She could feel it in her gut.

"Sort of. I want you to have the row homes. He wants Louie to have the row homes. We're at an impasse."

"I knew it had something to do with me."

"It's about more than that, really. And whatever is about you is not personal."

Pfft. How could it not be? If Alan Perrault liked her and respected her, he wouldn't be doing this. She would bet he never came close to freezing Stuart out over Trish. *Creep.* But that creep was Stuart's father, and she was … what? God, if she couldn't name it she certainly didn't deserve to come before his family.

"You should go to brunch," she said. "Apologize for lying to your mother. Make things right with your father."

"I can't do that."

"Why?"

"Because to make things right with my father, I'm going to have to screw things up with you." He took her hand and pulled her to him. "I don't want to do that."

She bit her quivering lip. "I don't want you to do that either."

"Good." He cupped her face and brushed his lips against hers. "Then, I'm not going to brunch. But …" he kissed her again. "If the offer still stands and your mother approves, I'll go to dinner with you."

•••

He'd missed another opportunity to come completely clean to Angie. He'd wanted to. He'd tried. Sort of. But she'd been so upset over the little bit he'd told her that he'd only wanted to calm her down.

And now, he was two hours into Sunday dinner with her family, the last place in the world he could find a quiet moment with her.

"That man needs another beer," said Angie's cousin Vin. The guy was bigger and more threatening than Tony, but he managed to accept Stuart being here.

Before he could blink, another bottle was in front of him. This family had the market on hospitality cornered. And, man, could Mrs. Corcarelli cook. He wished he'd worn sweatpants.

"Oh God, no," Angie said. "Not the photo box."

There was laughter all around the table.

"Are there nudie pics of Ange in there?" asked an older kid Stuart couldn't name.

"No," said Mrs. Corcarelli. "At least I don't think so. Maybe one or two of her in a diaper at the lake."

He laughed, too.

"You're really going to crucify me like this?"

"Honey, I've waited a long time for you to bring someone to dinner."

He was trying not to dwell on the significance of that. Meeting the family. It was an unexpected step. But, it wasn't entirely uncomfortable.

"Oh my God! Is that my first communion?" Angie grabbed a photo from her mother's hand. "Why did you cut my hair like that? I look like I belong on a paint can."

He leaned over. "Let me see."

"No. You'll never look at me the same way again." But she was laughing, and her eyes were sparkling, and he couldn't imagine looking at her any way but this way ever again.

Maybe he was falling in love with her. His chest sort of ached when he thought about it. Ached in a good way.

"Here. You can see this one. Prom."

"She's only showing you that because her cha-chas are hanging out," said one of the older woman across the table. Aunt Connie, maybe?

"Cha-chas?" Angie howled. "You still call them that?"

The woman nodded. "And hoo ha. Yes, indeed. A woman needs to respect her parts."

"Jesus, Ma," Vin said. "My ears don't want to hear about your parts."

Yep, Connie.

She smacked her son with the hand that wasn't bandaged. "Do not take God's name in vain. You're old enough to know better."

"And you're old enough to call them breasts and vagina," Angie said.

"Oh for crying out loud," said a gruff man at the other end of the table. "I'm going to find something on TV."

More laughter.

Finally he got a chance to look at the picture in his hand. She was gorgeous. Sultry and sexy beyond anything an eighteen-year-old should be. The guy next to her looked like a punk, and he had the urge to rip the picture in half, cutting the guy out of her memory.

"Nice, huh?" she asked, eyes still sparkling. "It took me three months to learn to walk in those heels. Nowhere near as comfortable as my work boots."

"I like your work boots."

She grinned and then shocked him with a kiss. In front of her family.

His face heated, but he was smiling like a loon.

"Oh! Pasquale," someone said.

When he looked up, Mrs. Corcarelli was teary-eyed and staring at a photograph.

"Let me see." Angie took the picture and held it tilted enough so that he could see, too.

The color had faded, but the image was of a man and a little girl standing in front of a white colonial house.

"I remember that house," Angie said. "It's in Beechview. That was the summer between fifth and sixth grade. He let me come to work with him every morning, and I ran tools back and forth from the tucks and kept the water jugs filled. Until the very end. He let me hammer my first, official nail. It was the last nail of the project. God, I miss him."

He reached beneath the table and smoothed a hand over her thigh.

And when her hand covered his, he was pretty damn sure there was no falling about it—he loved her.

He just didn't have a clue what to do about it.

Chapter Fourteen

Life was full of choices. Normally, Stuart made his with the help of a pen and paper and pros vs. cons. But where had that gotten him really? It hadn't saved his ass in Paris, and it hadn't done a damn thing for his social life. On the other hand, letting loose had gotten him Angie. So, he would go with that. Throw caution to the wind. Let the chips fall where they may.

He'd probably end up with an ulcer.

Monday morning. His first day back at work after taking a week off. *Time to face the music.* No doubt, it wouldn't be pretty.

"Morning, Kate."

His secretary looked up from the foam cup of coffee she'd been stirring and smiled. "Good morning. Are you rested after your vacation?"

He wished. "I had a nice break, yes."

"Excellent. Oh, your father said if you came in today he wanted to see you first thing."

Of course he did.

Stuart didn't rush over. He dropped his bag in his office and made a few calls, and then he wandered down the hall toward Ethan's office. It wouldn't hurt to know what he was walking into.

"He's out until this afternoon," Penny, Ethan's secretary, said.

So much for getting the scoop ahead of time. Not that he expected Ethan to tell him everything. But something was better than nothing.

When he couldn't put it off any longer, he walked into his father's office. "You wanted to see me?"

"I'm taking you off the highway project."

So much for pleasantries.

He closed his eyes and let that sink in. It didn't feel as lousy as he'd feared it would. Oh, it hurt, mostly because he could imagine Ethan's satisfaction over hearing it, but it didn't crush him.

"Your inability to do what was requested of you in regard to the sale of the Hazlett Street properties left me no choice."

He didn't try to tamp the anger when he felt it. "Oh, let's call it like it is, Dad. I wouldn't manipulate Angie into backing out, so you're pouting, and you're punishing me. She deserves those houses. She'd been trying to get them long before Ethan brought Louie to sniff around."

His father nodded. "Okay, since we're calling it like we see it, son, let me say something I've been holding in for a while now. I'm afraid you're not cut out for this business and you never will be. You can't make the tough decisions. In fact, it takes you too long to make any decision. I thought I could make you gutsier by putting you head to head with Ethan, that some of him would rub off on you, but even that didn't work." His father's forehead wrinkled, and the corners of his mouth drooped. "I don't know what else to do."

Give me another chance. He almost spoke the plea aloud, expecting the guilt and shame to kick in like autopilot, but surprisingly, he felt something else—relief that lording over this project wouldn't be his problem anymore. "I'm sorry I disappointed you again," he said instead.

His father shrugged. "I'm sorry too. I'll get over it, and maybe in time you can try a big project again. Maybe."

"No thanks," Stuart said. The impulsive words caught him by surprise.

Apparently they surprised his father, too. The man's eyes widened. "I get the feeling there's more you want to say."

There was, and this time he wasn't going to miss his chance to say it.

"I'm not happy here," he said. "I spent my time off at the Build Together Pittsburgh office, and I've realized I care about being there more than I ever cared about being here. Ethan's right. To be the best at a job you have to care the most." He cleared his throat. "So I quit."

His father folded his arms across his chest and his nostrils flared. "This is one time when you should really, really think before you act. Be careful of overly emotional decisions, son. They have a way of coming back to bite you. It's a lot easier walking away than it is crawling back."

True, but even so, Stuart stood straighter. "I won't be crawling back. I know what makes me happy now, and I'm going to run with that. I'm going to run with my charity … and Angie."

"It comes down to her, doesn't it?" His father exhaled loudly, and as he did, the anger he'd worn a moment ago disappeared. "Your mother saw that one coming. Seems I shot myself in the foot." He rounded his desk to grip Stuart by the shoulder, giving a good shake. "I wish you well, son. I do. I just can't help but think you're making a mistake."

If he was, it wouldn't be his first. If he wasn't, he had a lot to gain.

And this time, he didn't need to make a list of pros and cons to prove it.

• • •

"So you brought Stuart to Sunday dinner?" Trish asked.

"I don't want to talk about this if it's going to upset you." *Or me.* Angie wasn't in the mood to watch her mouth or hold her temper. Today had been another round of short-handed work crews and bad news at the flip.

"Do you see this bump, woman? Another man put it there. The man I love, who just so happens to be your brother. Why would I be upset about you being with Stu?"

"I don't know. Maybe because you still call him Stu." It bothered her. It did. She'd never heard anybody but Trish call him Stu—not even his parents. *Cripes.* Not only was she short-fused, she'd become territorial.

Trish laughed. "It's habit. Honest. I'll stop."

She exhaled more of the stress from her day and managed a smile. "No worries. I'm just glad you're talking to me. I figured Tony had plenty of time to turn you against me."

"Nah. Tony's never been rational where Stu … art is concerned."

"Nice catch."

"Thank you. And don't worry about your brother. I talked to him, and I'll keep talking to him until he sees what a butt he's being."

A nurse walked into the room and messed with the machine at Trish's head. "Looking good," the woman said. "Two more weeks and we can disconnect you and let nature take its course."

"You hear that?" Trish directed her voice toward her belly.

"God, that's such a long time to be in bed."

Trish nodded. "Tell me about it. I've already been in bed for two weeks."

A ruckus sounded in the hallway, and then Angelina burst into the room with a balloon in one hand and a piece of construction paper in the other. "Mommy! We brought presents."

Tony looked at Angie and then looked away, helping his daughter onto the bed.

"Hi, Princess," Trish said.

"Watch Mommy's belly." Tony glanced at Angie again.

"Hey, Tone," she said.

He nodded. It was better than nothing.

"Did you see Auntie Angie?" Trish nudged Angelina.

"Hi, Auntie."

Angie loved those little, flappy-fingered waves. "Hi, Princess."

"Where's the guy?" Angelina asked.

"What g …?" Crap.

"Great," Tony said. "Apparently, she's like the rest of the family thinking he belongs with you."

The rest of the family thought she and Stuart belonged together? All her mother had said was that he seemed like a nice man.

"Nothing wrong with that," Trish said, smiling.

And even though Tony huffed, he didn't look half as angry as she'd expected him to be.

It didn't take long for Angelina to get antsy in the small room, so Tony took her for a walk to the cafeteria, leaving Angie and Trish to discuss business.

The Fox Chapel house was finished, and the family would be moving in on Friday. The South Fayette kitchen was cutting it close to deadline after the cabinet mishap. A floor refinishing started up in Cranberry, and an addition set to be framed early next week.

"How's the flip going?" Trish asked.

"I'm starting to think it's a money pit. I know if you do enough of them, you're bound to run into one that isn't easy, but this is not the time to run into that one. I don't know how I'm going to afford renovating those row houses if I keep sinking more and more money into this place on the South Side."

"Stuart will lend you the money."

"God, no. I would never ask him to do that, especially after what I just found out. His father is against me purchasing the row homes." She shook her head. "I've caused enough trouble in that family already."

"Oh, that family has always been troubled. I don't know how Stuart came from them. Although, Mary isn't bad."

No, Stuart's mother wasn't bad—just a little pushy in the grandchild department. Weren't all mothers, though? And grandmothers. Nonna's pushiness had led to this. She stared at Trish's belly. *Two more weeks, little one. You can do it.*

"Have you thought of a name yet?" she asked.

"Uh, actually, yes, we have. I thought maybe Tony would've told you."

She shook her head. "We haven't really been talking lately."

"Well, then I'll tell you. Pasquale Antonio, which would make him a junior, so we'll call him PJ."

Pasquale. A lump of tears formed in her throat and her hands grew clammy. They were naming the baby after her dad. Why wouldn't they? They'd named Angelina after Nonna.

And she thought buying some row homes that may or may not have anything to do with her father was the way to honor his memory. Boy, that paled in comparison to naming a kid after him.

She grabbed Trish's hand. "I think that's awesome. Perfect, actually." Every time she called her nephew by his name, she'd think of her father.

That's all she really ever wanted ... reminders of him, so she wouldn't forget.

Again, she thought about the row houses. Maybe she shouldn't buy them. If family came first, then she needed to treat them better than putting the company into more debt and taking on more work than they could handle. She also shouldn't be wedging herself between Stuart and his father, especially if she thought there was the slightest chance for a future with him.

There were other ways to honor a memory.

A rush of emotion carried her to her feet. "I gotta make a phone call."

• • •

Stuart hung up the phone, dropped his head to the back of the armchair, and smiled at the ceiling. Simon Cross had said Angie's bid was going to be accepted officially at a meeting tomorrow morning. *Take that Dad, Ethan, and Louie.* It was a nice way to end the day.

Then Angie called, and that was even better.

"I like your bed," she said.

"It likes you, too."

"Then it wouldn't mind seeing me again, say, in fifteen minutes?"

"It wouldn't mind at all. In fact, I have something to tell you." Two things actually. Three things if he ever decided telling her he loved her was the smart thing to do.

"That's funny. I have something to tell you, too."

What if she loved him back? He shook his head and palmed his forehead. She was probably going to tell him what he already knew. Maybe Simon or Jana had called her, too.

Ten minutes later, he was standing at his front door watching her hop out of the truck. He grinned. "Not taking anything away from that black dress you wore the other night, but there's something very sexy about a woman in work boots and jeans."

"Really?" She sauntered toward him. "Well, there's something very sexy about a man in wrinkled dress clothes." She curled her fingers into the open collar of his shirt. "What happened to your tie?"

"It's hanging around the bed post, waiting for you."

"Excellent." She yanked the shirttails from his pants and covered his mouth with hers.

"So, no small talk about our day?" he teased, even as his hands grabbed hold of her ass and pulled her against him.

"No." She unbuttoned and unzipped him.

He licked a path up her neck even as he kicked the door closed, and then he pressed her against it. "Then, I guess you won't get to hear my exciting news."

She stopped fishing around in his pants. "What exciting news?"

He smirked and brushed a thumb across her nipple. "The city is going to accept your offer. Tomorrow morning there will be a meeting, and then I imagine they'll contact you. Unless they've already contacted you."

Her face twisted. "How do you know this?"

"I got a call from Simon Cross about twenty minutes ago."

"No." She pushed him away and slipped out from between him and the door. "I just left a message on Jana Wright's voicemail. I withdrew my name."

His eyes widened, and an ice pick pain split his head in two. "You did what?"

She wandered into his living room shaking her head. "I don't want those houses anymore."

He did not understand. Things that seemed so damn clear a few hours ago fogged up with so much rabid emotion he couldn't recognize them. So what she was telling him was he'd spent the last few weeks going against his family, when ultimately he needn't have bothered? And now, she didn't even want the homes for which he'd helped her fight?

"Are you mad at me?" she asked. "I can't tell."

"I'm confused." Hell, thirty seconds ago he was anticipating one heck of an orgasm. Now, he felt like someone had bludgeoned him.

"Let me explain." She sat in an armchair and gnawed her bottom lip. "This goes way back to when I was apprenticing under my dad. We used to drive around town from job to job, and he would point out all the houses he'd worked on over the years. Well, those row homes on Hazlett Street look just like ones he showed me once. He said he'd learned his craft there. I couldn't let a piece of my father's history be destroyed. There's not much of him left in the world, you know? I mean there's me and Tony, but besides that ..." she shrugged.

"Anyhow, I'd been trying to buy those homes for months, and the city employees I talked to kept saying I could as soon as the property was removed from the tax rolls, but nobody told me when that happened, and that led me to you, and ..." She looked at him, really looked at him for the first time since she started talking, and a small smile curved her lips. "I'm glad it brought me to you. I am." But then she shook her head and the smile faded. "It's just that now Trish can't leave the hospital until the baby is born, which means she can't work, and I'm the most logical person to cover for her. But I have my company, too. You know this flip is draining me. Time is money. I can't get behind there. I have to pay my crew. They're family. Family first. See? I can't possibly do it all, especially since I don't even have proof that my father had anything to do with those houses in the first place."

He couldn't wrap his mind around all of it. She'd gone after the row homes because she *thought* her father had worked on them—she didn't have proof! It was an emotional reason to act, and now she was bailing because she was feeling overwhelmed. More emotion. This was not good business. Not to mention it was a shitty way to pay him back for all he'd done for her. Had he known this was coming, he could've played it off in a way that would have reflected positively on him. He wouldn't have had to pull her off if she was going to pull herself off. Hell, he could've stayed as lead on the highway project. He could've weathered Ethan's attempts to topple him. He could've ...

"Say something," she said.

What? Where should he even start? He sat in the armchair across from her. "Let me get this straight. I've stood behind you, alienated my family, and annihilated my career so you could end up making a rash, emotional decision that makes me look like a fool."

Her face darkened. "No. No, it's not like that. Not at all."

"How can you say that? You were emotional about this from the moment you walked into my office and demanded I move the highway." He laughed. "Listen to that. You didn't even own that property, and you demanded I move the highway. This project had nothing to do with you. You were so damn emotional my father insisted I call you and smooth things over. Even he was scared of the chaos you could cause. And look, I hate to admit it, but he had a point."

If her eyes had been lasers, he'd have been fried dead in his chair. "Your father made you call me? Of course he did. And of course you did it. You took me to dinner. You turned on the charm. You had me right where you wanted me. Keep quiet, Angie. Buy the houses and move them, Angie. Do this, Angie. Do that. Ha! The big bad emotional bitch you were all so worried about was tamed by a cold, calculating manipulator. I bet you made a list for that. And now you can frame it." She jumped up from her seat and stalked to the door. "God, and you wonder why I don't trust men. Let me tell you something. The decisions I made about those houses were not emotional decisions … but this one is."

She left with a hearty slam of the door.

Chapter Fifteen

When the bottom fell out from under everything, a girl needed her mother—and chocolate.

"You're not emotional; you're passionate," Angie's mother said.

They sat on the couch stuffing their faces with Perugina Baci.

"Thank you." An hour after slamming the door on Stuart, she was feeling a little bit better, but nowhere near as sure of herself as she wanted to feel. "Maybe he had a point. Maybe I shouldn't have called Jana on a whim like that. Maybe I should've told him first."

Why? So he could've talked her out of what she knew was the right thing to do so he could save face with his family?

But she couldn't imagine him doing that. Not the man she knew. The man who was sitting in that chair when she left was shocked and confused. If he hadn't been—if she'd talked to him first and thought this through—she could've totally seen him understanding and acknowledging that she had legitimate business concerns. He still may have been a little angry when he found out her reason for wanting those properties was, well, flimsy, but he would've helped her come up with a plan to proceed.

God, he was right; she'd made an emotional decision in the first place, and she'd made a giant mess of everything.

"It's always nice to have someone you can trust to bounce things off of," her mother said. "That's what I miss most about your father. That and his bear hugs."

Stuart gave great hugs, too. But that wasn't going to fix anything now.

She was so confused. Sure, she'd made an emotional decision, but he'd gone along with his father's demand to schmooze her.

How could she trust that anything that had happened between them hadn't been at least partially faked?

"His father made him call me and take me to dinner all those weeks ago," she said. "That bothers me. What if he was faking everything to save a business deal? What if what happened between us meant more to me than it did to him?"

"Well, it may have started out as a way to appease his father, but how it started out is less important than how it ended up. You were there, and you're a smart woman. I think you would've noticed if he was faking the important stuff." Her mother slipped an arm around her shoulders and squeezed. "He wasn't faking the way he looked at you during dinner. But don't take my word for it. You should ask him what it meant to him." She squeezed again. "And before you do that, you should ask yourself what it meant to you. You've never brought a man to Sunday dinner before."

Nope. She'd never wanted to. Had never even thought of it. Had never really thought about marriage and kids before Stuart, either. Maybe that made her a fool. Because she could see it still. Waking up to him every morning. Buying a house they could renovate together. Sitting at a big dining table teaching their kids to build stick houses. Working together at BTP.

What had it meant to her? Everything.

She hung her head. "I guess the more time we spent together, the more I thought maybe this could be it."

"It still could be. All couples fight. Your father and I broke up for two weeks during our engagement because Nonna stopped talking to him over the fact that I wasn't going to become Catholic. He begged me to convert, but I couldn't go against my family like that. So we broke up. And we were miserable. Miserable enough that religion didn't seem to matter anymore. Family opinion didn't seem to matter anymore, either. He said he wanted me. I said I wanted him. And we both said to hell with everything else."

She laughed. Her mother wasn't big on the swear words the rest of the family threw around so easily. "I didn't know that. I mean I knew not being Catholic was an issue, but I didn't know you broke up. I'm so glad you got back together." She dropped her head to her mother's shoulder. "But … I'm not sure that relates to me. Stuart hasn't proposed. Not even close. I'm getting way ahead of myself. See? I am too emotional for my own good."

"Passionate. And it makes you extra special. Any man who doesn't see that isn't the right man for you."

She closed her eyes as she nodded, but it hurt to think that Stuart might not be the right one. "I think I love him."

"I think you do, too."

"What do I do?"

"You tell him. If he loves you, too, then to hell with everything else. And if he doesn't, then he's a damn fool."

• • •

Stuart rolled over and reached for Angie. When his hand met cold sheets, he opened his eyes to the early morning sunshine. He'd barely slept.

God, he hated this bed. So damn uncomfortable.

He headed to the shower, and for a split second expected to find her there. Empty.

He hated this shower. Too damn big.

He skipped coffee and breakfast at his counter in favor of getting an early start at BTP's Dormont headquarters.

On his way into town, his phone rang.

"Can you bring the utilities PowerPoint to the three o'clock meeting?" Ethan asked.

What? "Why would I do that? I quit."

"Excuse me?"

"Didn't Dad tell you? I walked into his office yesterday, and I quit."

"Uh, no. Why would you do that?"

"Because I'm tired of the games. I want to focus on BTP." And Angie.

He should've gone after her, but she'd hurled that line about trusting men at him with such conviction, he couldn't think of anything that would make her believe he shouldn't be lumped into that category.

"Wow. I'm speechless."

"Except you just *told* me you were speechless, so you're not. Come on, admit it. This makes you happy."

"Only if you're happy. We might be dysfunctional, but we're family. Honestly, I just expected he'd name us co-CEOs someday, and we'd be locking horns until we were old and gray."

It didn't sound appealing, but the fact that Ethan saw a future where they could've shared the title was touching.

"Hey," Ethan continued. "I'll talk to you later. That's Louie on the other line."

Probably to tell him his bid had been accepted.

Stuart was more than willing not to deal with the drama anymore. Last night, he'd lost sight of that. All he could think of was that he'd unnecessarily given up everything. But that wasn't accurate. At all. Ten minutes after Angie had left, he'd remembered the real reason he'd left the family business. He wanted to do what made him happy.

Traffic slowed until it was bumper to bumper. Maybe it was a wreck. Eventually, he came upon a detour sign. *Where did this come from?* He'd driven the Churchill to Dormont route all last week, and there wasn't a single notice that construction would be coming. Looked like another city official dropped the ball on required notification.

And it looked like he was going to be taking the scenic route through Beechview.

He fiddled with the radio. When the snail's pace turned to a complete halt, he checked emails. And then, when he had nothing better to do, he took in his surroundings.

He'd never been here before. Lots of older homes in need of TLC. But it was charming. With its proximity to the city, the neighborhood could be ripe for resurgence. Had Angie ever looked for houses to rehab here?

He looked at his phone. If he called her, would she pick up? Probably not. He called her anyway.

Her voice filled his car. "Hi, you've reached Angela Corcarelli and Corcarelli Carpentry Company. Leave me a message, and I'll get back to you soon."

"Angie, it's me. I'm sorry about last night. Please, give me a chance to apologize and explain."

He needed more than words, though, didn't he?

Further up the road, a bright green "for sale" sign caught his eye. It was stuck in the patchy front lawn of a dirty, white colonial. His skin hummed, and his eyes widened. *No way.* That house looked like the one he'd seen in a photograph at Sunday dinner. Angie and her father had been standing in front of a house that looked an awful lot like this. It couldn't be. Wishful thinking.

But what if it was the same house?

Then it was fate, and he was supposed to here, stuck in this detour, driving by this house, because seeing this place again would mean the world to the woman he loved. He had to do something about it.

He pulled into the driveway and picked up his phone.

It'd been years since he'd called Trish.

"Oh my God," she said. "How are you?"

"Don't worry about me! How are you? You're stuck in the hospital."

"True, but I'm good. Hopeful. Everyone is."

"Excellent." He stared up at the house that looked vacant. "Listen, is Tony there?"

Silence.

"I know that's probably the last thing you expected to hear me say, but I need to talk to him. It's important, and I don't have his number."

"Why didn't you ask Angie for his number?"

"We, well … it's complicated. Things kind of fell apart last night, and I'm trying to find a way to put them back together."

He must've said the right thing, because ten seconds after they hung up, Trish texted him Tony's contact information.

The guy wasn't exactly happy to hear from him. "Where'd you get my number?"

"From your wife." Those were loaded words.

"Why are you calling my wife?"

"For your number. Listen, do we have to keep doing this? I'm not a threat, man. I don't want to be a threat." *Tell him why.* "I'm in love with your sister."

"Jesus H. Christ."

"Yeah, I figured you wouldn't be thrilled, but hey, look at it this way. At least I'm not in love with your wife."

He expected to be hung up on, instead Tony said, "True."

It was one word, but it seemed to carry a lot of weight. Maybe something had shifted between them.

"Listen, I'm sitting in front of a house in Beechview on …" he craned his neck to see if he could find a street sign, and then he fiddled with his GPS. "I have no idea where I am, but it's a white colonial. I'm pretty sure it's a house I saw in a picture at your mom's. Your father and sister were standing in front of it, and she said it was the first nail she drove in an actual project. Do you remember that house?"

"Yeah. Sure do. I was there, too, but while she was working, I was hanging out at this shop on the corner that sold candy and had a hot chick working the register."

"Angie was what? Ten? Eleven? How old were you?"

"Old enough to recognize a great pair of … legs."

Stuart smiled as he craned his neck to look down the block. "What did the place look like?"

"The house?"

"No, the store."

"Eh, I don't remember. It had a screen door that closed too fast. I remember that part. I had to hurry up and get through it before it hit me in the ass."

Worthless information. He got out of the car and took off on foot. "You don't remember the name of the store?"

"Nope."

"Was the parking lot big or small?"

"Don't know. But there was a Pepsi cooler right outside the door. I used to get yelled at by Mr. Brizicki for sitting on it."

He was at the end of the block now, and ready to give up, when a truck moved out of the way and revealed a yellowing sign with a faded B. As in Brizicki. "B's Grocery?"

"Bingo."

Yes! It was boarded up, but it was there, and so was the rusted Pepsi cooler. "Thanks, man. I've got to go."

"Hey, wait. One thing. Since you got my number, you can stop calling my wife, right?"

He chuckled. "If this works, I can stop calling you, too, because I'll be back to calling your sister instead."

Chapter Sixteen

On a whim, Angie pulled into The Perrault Group parking garage. She had to tell him. She had to get it off her chest. And then, she was going to ask him if he felt the same, because she couldn't take another night of staring at the ceiling, wondering what to do next.

This could backfire. She hopped out of her truck anyway. *This could backfire in front of his father and brother.* Which made her stomach flip, but she squared her shoulders and opened the front door anyway.

"Can I help you?" asked the librarian-like woman who she recognized from the last time she'd stormed Stuart's office.

"I'm here to see …"

"Angie?"

She turned to see Mr. Perrault walking toward her.

"What can I help you with today?" he asked.

For a man who'd been rooting for her to fail, he still managed to pull off cordial. "Hi, Mr. Perrault. I'm here to see Stuart."

He looked at the receptionist and smiled. "Follow me, Angie."

A personal escort? Talk about nerve-racking. But she could use this time to lay some groundwork. She loved his son, and she hoped his son loved her. And she hoped they had a future together.

"I'm sure you've heard I'm not interested in buying the row homes anymore." She spoke to his back.

"Yes. I've heard that."

"I'm sure you're happy about it. I know you wanted to see someone else's offer accepted."

He glanced at her. "Nothing personal. Business is business."

"Right. Except, when you try to get ahead in business by encouraging someone to have a personal relationship with the competition, the lines get blurred."

He stopped at a door with his name on a silver plaque and looked at her. "Young lady, I don't know what my son has told you, but apparently he hasn't told you everything. Did I ask him to take you out and sway your decisions? Yes. Did it work? No. You're here, looking for him, but he quit ... days ago."

"What?" Why hadn't he told her that? Then again, she hadn't exactly given him much of a chance to tell her. She'd slammed his door. She hadn't looked back. And now she wasn't answering his calls.

"All I've ever asked of him was to put the business first," Mr. Perrault said. "And when he had the chance to do so, he chose you."

Oh my God. No wonder he'd been so shocked by what she'd done. He had still been reeling from what *he'd* done.

He'd quit. For her. Maybe he loved her, too.

"Do you know where he is?" she asked.

"Probably at his do-gooder headquarters in Dormont."

"Thank you," she called as she backed her way down the hallway. In a weird way, she meant it. Without Mr. Perrault's lack of business scruples, Stuart may have never asked her out in the first place.

Unfortunately, she couldn't head straight to the BTP office. She had to drive over to the South Side and check in at the flip. She called Stuart on her way, but he didn't answer.

She left a message: *Hey, it's me. I ... can't believe you quit.*

There was no way she was going to tell him she loved him on an answering machine, even if the words were beating out of her chest.

I'm sorry, too. Call me.

Maybe by the time he called her back she'd have figured out the right way to tell him she loved him. She'd said some things last night that she wished she could take back, and she hadn't said some things she should have. She'd learned her lesson. This time, she was going to think things through. Sometimes it paid to plan things out. Not that she needed a list.

She tried to lose herself in the work at the flip, but Stuart was never completely out of her mind.

"Ange, I wrote a number on the doorjamb right below the upper flange," Jesse said about a half hour after she'd walked through the door. "Can you tell me what it is?"

She squinted at the light pencil written on white paint. "Thirty-seven and one-fourth."

"Thanks."

Dante walked into the room carrying two pieces of drywall. Neither was very big, but one looked kind of awkward.

"Pitch or keep?" he asked. "They're leftovers from the patch in the upstairs bath. I was going to keep this one and paint something on it, but who am I kidding? I'm no artist. I just like the look of clean drywall."

"Me, too." She might prefer wood, but she got the whole blank slate thing. "Give me one. I'll help you carry them to the dumpster."

As she walked along behind him, staring at the stark white surface, she imagined the kind of painting she'd create. Stick figures. That was about all she was good for. But she couldn't ignore the feeling that something belonged on this plasterboard. Words? Like, *I love you, Stuart?* Cheesy. Maybe.

"On second thought, I'm going to save this one," she said.

She almost pitched it again when she reached the South Fayette kitchen. She was not going to write *I love you* on a piece of drywall. Then what? Drive over to his house and prop it outside his front door? Again, cheesy. And nowhere near the serious impression she wanted to make. She needed him to understand how much thought she'd put into this. He valued thought. That's why he made all those lists. And she valued him.

The lists. She could make a list. Pros and cons of loving Stuart. It could be a little tongue in cheek, which would help take the sting out of any possible negative reaction, but it would be the honest-to-God truth, too.

When lunch rolled around, she sat in her truck with the piece of drywall propped against the steering wheel and a Sharpie in her hand. A list of pros had been running through her head since she'd come up with the dumb idea.

Just write something. She could always pitch it if it ended up looking as goofy as it sounded.

She wrote, *All the Reasons I Love Stuart*, and cringed. There had to be something better than that … but it was written in permanent ink.

Ugh.

She pushed on, pretty sure this was headed for the trash, glancing out the windows every now and then just to make sure nobody was going to find her writing things like *the sex* and *the showers.*

But hey, she was smiling after that.

The rest of the list spilled out of her and onto the chalky surface.

- The construction knowledge
- Not eating alone at the counter anymore
- Someone to build with
- Someone to talk to
- Someone to take to Sunday dinner

Her letters were big and loopy. The lines slanted. God, even her writing was an emotional mess. Scratch that, passionate. Whatever she called it, she'd almost run out of space. Room for one more thing.

She wrote, "Someone to hold my ladder."

Her eyes burned. *Don't cry, dork.* She rubbed away the sting. There was nothing to cry about right now. He either loved her and wouldn't think this was half as sappy as she did, or he didn't love her, and she should save her tears for that.

When her phone rang, she jumped. *Tony.*

"Hey. What's up?"

"Contractions started again. But I don't want to freak everyone out, because there's a chance they will stop, so I'm just telling you right now. I had to tell someone. I'm, uh, freaking out myself."

Hadn't Trish said they wanted two more weeks? This couldn't be good.

"The doc said twenty-eight-weekers can make it, so, uh, if the contractions don't stop, and he comes now at thirty weeks, he's gonna be good. Right?"

"Heck yeah." She dumped the drywall to the passenger-side floor. "I'll be right there. I'm coming to sit with you, Tone. Hang tight. We'll get through this together."

• • •

Stuart emerged from his realtor's office with an accepted offer on the Beechview colonial. He'd be back in one week to close. Paying in cash made things a whole lot easier, but all the money in the world couldn't help him settle on the best way to tell her what he'd done and why he'd done it.

This was either going to be the greatest gesture a man had ever made or the biggest flop.

And now he was dragging her mother into it.

"Hi, Stuart." Mrs. Corcarelli opened the door wearing the broadest smile. "I'm so glad you called me. Come in."

"I appreciate your help."

She closed the door behind him and then picked a propped-up envelope from a hutch. "Of course I'd help you. Although now you have me curious about why exactly you need this picture. I don't want to be nosy, but …" she wrinkled her nose, "I am."

"All mothers are. Mine included." When he'd called his mom to apologize for lying about being sick, she'd grilled him until he'd admitted he'd been spending serious time with Angie.

"Oh, I like your mother already." Her brows lifted. "Maybe someday we'll get to meet."

"Absolutely." Because if all went well, he would be a fixture in her daughter's life for a long, long time.

She handed him the envelope. "I put the prom picture in there, too. You can always cut the other guy out."

He laughed. "I like the way you think."

She grabbed hold of his hand. "And I like you. If I say much more than that, Angie would kill me. But you're a good man, and she's a good woman, and I hope you can make this work."

"Me too."

Somewhere in the distance, a phone rang, and Mrs. Corcarelli let go of his hand to wave it off. "You're not going to tell me what this is about, are you?"

He shook his head. *How do you tell a mother that you bought a house for her daughter without opening Pandora's box?* "I think it's better if I keep quiet for now."

A click sounded, and the room filled with an automated male voice. People still had answering machines?

"Probably the garage," she said. "My car's getting inspected."

Suddenly, Angie's voice filled the room. "*Arrgh!* You need to get a cell phone. Trish is going to have the baby. Cesarean section."

Mrs. Corcarelli rushed around the living room. "Where is that phone? I had it a little bit ago while I was talking to Connie. Sometimes I put it in strange places, because I'm not thinking."

Stuart helped her look. By the time they found it hidden behind a roll of paper towels in the kitchen, Angie's voice was long gone.

"I'll call her back." She was crying. "She'll have to come get me. I don't even have a car."

"I'll drive you."

It was a solemn drive. No more broad smiles and attempts to pry information from him. He lent her his cell phone, and listened while she called her sisters-in-law. At this rate, the hospital would need an entire wing to hold the Corcarelli family members who would be trickling in. It didn't surprise him that Angie was already there. She was emotional about her family. Passionate. And that wasn't anywhere near the liability he'd always thought it was.

In fact, it was one of many reasons why he loved her.

"No, honey. It's me."

Stuart glanced at Mrs. Corcarelli, who mouthed Angie and pointed at his phone.

"I'm calling from Stuart's phone," she said.

He figured she'd get around to making that call sooner or later.

"My car is in the garage … Angela, I'll explain when I get there. What's going on? I tried Tony, but he didn't answer his phone. Is he in the operating room? Well then, why didn't he answer my call?"

Stuart knew why. Tony had probably added his number to contacts so he could avoid all future calls if Stuart's name popped up. Maybe it was warped, but that made him smile.

"General anesthesia?" Mrs. Corcarelli made the sign of the cross.

He hoped Trish and the baby would be okay.

"Angie wants to talk to you."

This wasn't the way he wanted to talk to her, but he took the phone—and a breath—and said, "Hello."

"Thank you. For driving her. I don't know how that ended up happening, but thank you."

"You're welcome. I told you …" he flashed a look at her mother, "I'm here when you need me. Nothing has changed."

"Good. I want to say more, but not now."

"Understood." Again, he looked at her mother.

"Will you come in for a little bit when you drop off her off?"

"If you want me to."

"I do."

Then he'd be there.

• • •

Seeing her mother step into the waiting room with Stuart behind her was crazy. In a good way. He smiled at her, and at least half of the day's weight evaporated.

"Any update?" her mother asked.

"No." Tony's leg bounced like a jackhammer eating up cement. "I wish I could be in there; then I'd know. Damn general anesthesia."

Angie smoothed a hand over his thigh and patted until he calmed down. "They're going to be okay."

"Where's Dr. DeVign?" Stuart asked.

"They left for a medical conference in Hawaii yesterday," she said. "Trish's mom is trying to get a flight back today."

"Excuse me for a minute," Stuart replied, and then he stepped away from them.

Maybe he had to make a call or use the restroom.

Her mother hugged Tony, and then settled in the seat beside him.

"So how'd that happen?" Tony asked, jerking his head in the direction Stuart had taken.

Since he brought it up … "I'd like to know, too."

Her mother shrugged. "He was there when Angie left the message. I couldn't find the phone in time to answer. He offered to give me a ride. It really was very thoughtful of him."

Tony snorted. "I'm going to be seeing a lot more of him, huh?"

"I hope so," Angie said.

Five minutes later, he walked back into the waiting room with a nurse by his side.

"Mr. Corcarelli, will you come with me? We'll see if we can't get you some information about your wife."

Angie didn't miss the little nod Stuart tossed the nurse's way as she and Tony were leaving. "Did you have something to do with that?"

He shook his head. "Not really. Must've been time for an update."

She didn't believe him, but this time it was okay.

Aunt Connie and Vin showed up, and her mother moved closer to them to pass on what little detail she had.

Stuart sat, and Angie rocked against him. "I'm glad you're here."

He grabbed her hand. "I'm glad I'm here, too."

"I'm sorry."

"For what?"

"For slamming your door."

He chuckled. "Yes, you should've closed it quietly."

"I shouldn't have closed it at all. I should've listened to you, and then we should've talked it through, and then …" she laid her head on his shoulder and lifted her lips to his ear, "we should've had make-up sex."

"Oh, we will," he said, and he wrapped his arm around her.

She closed her eyes and thought about all the hours she'd spent in hospital waiting rooms. Between her father, her grandmother, and now Trish, she'd logged more than her fair share. But this time didn't seem so hopeless. Maybe it was a sign that Trish and PJ were going to be okay.

Stuart smoothed a hand up and down her arm.

Or maybe it was him.

Tony never came back to the waiting room. The same nurse who led him away returned to tell everyone the baby had been born and was being taken to NICU. Trish was still under the effects of the general anesthesia.

Of course, that was when Angie got a call from Jesse saying he thought he'd found black mold in the crawlspace at the flip.

"I'll go," Stuart said. "I can make a couple calls on my way over there, and maybe have my buddy, Dave, take a look at it. He does mold remediation for a living. You stay with your family."

Never. She'd never had support like this. "Okay."

She walked him out to his car. Hand in hand. Occasionally she thought about the piece of drywall. And then it hit her, the funny thing about lists was they weren't meant to be shared. They were just there for you to get your thoughts together, so you knew you were on the right track.

"I love you," she said. On the third floor of a hospital parking garage.

He smiled. "I love you, too." Then he cupped her face and pulled her lips to his.

She checked out, let everything else slip away except the warmth of his hands, the pressure of his mouth, and the scent of his skin.

"You owe me make-up sex," he whispered.

"Here?" A couple more kisses like that, and she could be persuaded.

He laughed. "No. Later."

"Okay."

"We have things to talk about, like why I was with your mother today."

"Yeah. I want the whole truth and nothing but the truth." She tugged on his tie.

"Oh, you'll get it. Along with something else."

He was talking about the makeup sex, wasn't he?

What else could there be?

Chapter Seventeen

It was late when Angie finally called Stuart and told him she was on her way over. Too late for him to tell her about the Beechview house in the slightly over-the-top way he planned to. *That* involved luring her there for a false estimate on some custom cabinetry. Maybe he could evade questions about why he was at her mother's until tomorrow, and put the plan into action then.

He sighed. Tomorrow would be tight. He needed to be at her South Side flip early in the morning for the mold remediation, and in the afternoon he had an important meeting with a potential corporate sponsor for the BTPKids program. Angie would be shuffling between projects, too, and then she'd want to spend some time at the hospital with Tony and Trish.

His plan wasn't going to work.

He would have to go rogue.

There was a time when straying from a plan would've been out of the question. Now, he was just so damn happy, he didn't care. He wanted to see her face when she saw the place—and he wanted to see it soon.

Her headlights shone through his living room window, and a wave of impulse sent him out the door.

He held up his hand to stop her from getting out of the truck, and then he jogged to the passenger side.

"What are you doing?" she asked, when he opened the door.

"I need you to take me someplace." But there was a piece of drywall in his way. He reached for it. "Can I throw this in back?"

"No." She lunged across the seat to reach it. "I'll, uh, tuck it behind here."

When she picked the board up off the floor, he saw writing. He could've sworn he'd seen *Stuart*.

He grabbed the trailing corner and attempted to flip it, but she resisted.

"What is this?" he asked.

"It's cheesy."

"Did I see my name?"

She nodded. "It's a list."

"And I'm on it? Am I naughty or nice?"

"Both. But it's not that kind of list. It's, well …" she flipped it writing-side up and laid it on the seat. "Just read it and get it over with."

"*All the Reasons I Love Stuart.*" He smiled. "That's cute."

"It's fricking cheesy. I thought making a list would show you I'd thought it through enough to be taken seriously. Ha ha."

He slid the board behind the bench seat and climbed into the truck. "I take you very seriously," he said. "And I'm going to prove it to you." He kissed her. "Now drive."

"Where?"

"Head west on 376."

She glanced at him as she put the truck in reverse. "Should I be worried?"

"Just trust me."

At the end of his driveway she stopped the truck and looked at him long and hard. "I do trust you. I really do."

"Good." He leaned over and kissed her again. "I won't ever do anything to make you regret it."

She drove on.

He gave turn-by-turn directions, and in between, they talked about everything from Trish and Baby PJ—who was stable but facing several weeks in the NICU—to the mold and BTP.

"We're heading toward Dormont. Are you taking me to the office?" She gasped. "Did you get BTPKids fully funded? Did you give me a corner office with my name on a plaque?"

He loved that she was as excited about the idea as he was.

"That meeting is tomorrow. If it's a go, you'll be the first to know."

She smiled. "It's going to be a go, because it's an awesome idea."

"And you inspired it."

"I don't know about that."

He knew. She inspired him. Not only did he love her, but he needed her. She made him a better man. As soon as everything calmed down, he was going to ask her to marry him.

"Turn here," he said, unable to hide his enthusiasm.

"Okay. Now, I'm really confused. Who lives in Beechview?"

He shrugged. "I don't know. But slow down, and turn left up here."

Her headlights bounced back at them off the shiny *For Sale* sign that had a bright *Under Contract* banner hanging from the bottom.

"Pull into the driveway."

She looked at him, and her brows furrowed. "Who lives here?"

"Just pull into the driveway."

When she did, he unbuckled his seatbelt and leaned forward for a better look. The headlights only illuminated a portion of the house, but it was enough that he hoped she could fully appreciate it.

"Do you recognize this place?"

She leaned forward, too, brows still furrowed. "I don't know. Maybe there's something familiar. It's hard to tell in the dark."

He opened his door just a crack so the interior light shone, and then he reached into his pocket and pulled out the picture Mrs. Corcarelli had given him.

"Here," he said, as he passed the photo to her. "Do you recognize it now?"

Dead silence. Not even a breath. Her hand was shaking so badly he didn't know how she could see the photograph.

But then she looked up at the house again, and he saw her tears.

"I bought it," he whispered. "For you."

•••

Angie couldn't see past her tears. She'd worked on this house with her dad. And she had the proof in her hands. She also had a man beside her who would make something like this happen. Was she dreaming?

"You bought this house for me?"

He nodded, the sweetest smile on his face.

Reality set in. "Oh my God! Stuart, that's so much money."

"You're worth it."

"But you just quit your job. You're trying to expand your nonprofit. I don't want to sound ungrateful, but I'm worried you … well, I'm worried you made an emotional decision that you'll regret. I mean, what if you don't get a return on your investment? What if I can't part with it when I'm done renovating it?" She looked at the house and then at the photograph again. "Yeah, I can tell you right now I'll never be able to sell this house."

He hooked a finger beneath her chin and lifted her face. "I know that. And I'm not worried about getting a return on my investment. I have plenty of money, Angie. One thing my parents did right was set their sons up very well. The house is yours, free and clear."

She gasped. "Thank you!" Wrapping her arms around his neck, she squeezed him until he reached up to loosen her grip.

"So you're happy?" he asked. "I wasn't sure for a minute there."

"God, yes! I'm happier than I've been in a long time. Because of you." She kissed him. "Thank you. Thank you. Thank you."

He smiled as he wiped away her tears with soft sweeps of his thumbs. "This is why I was at your mother's house when you called about Trish and the baby. I had a plan to frame the photograph and have it waiting on the mantel when you walked in. Trish was going to give you the address and tell you to stop over for an estimate. But, I couldn't make that happen for obvious reasons, and I didn't want to wait. So here we are."

His words echoed in her head as she gazed into his sparkling eyes. Where were they exactly? And she didn't mean Beechview.

He loved her. She loved him. He'd bought her a house.

They were standing on the edge of a future together.

She propped the photograph on the dashboard, smiled at her father's image, and then looked at Stuart. "I want us to renovate this house together. Just you and me. We can use crews when we have no choice, but …" she took his hands in hers and lifted them to her mouth, "I want these hands to do most of the work. I want the old memories to mix with the new ones."

He kissed her knuckles as she kissed his. "Deal. Buying this house may have been an emotional decision, but it was the best decision I've ever made. Well, next to falling in love with you."

Through laughter and tears she glanced at the photo again. "I can't help but think my father had something to do with this. From the beginning I was looking for a way to stay close to him, and I found it. I found you, too."

Stuart glanced at the roof of the truck. "Mr. Corcarelli, if you're up there watching, thank you. Now, please, close your eyes so I can *really* kiss your daughter."

Her laughter was silenced with his lips, then his tongue, then his hands combing through her hair.

Was she happy? She was delirious.

Life couldn't get any better than this, Angie thought.

• • •

But she was wrong.

Three months later, while she was standing at the top of a ladder putting up crown molding in the living room, she heard Stuart yell from the kitchen, "We should get going so we can shower and change before we head to Tony and Trish's for PJ's coming home party."

"One more strip," she yelled back.

When she finished, he was standing at the bottom, one foot on the lowest rung, both hands on the rails. Holding her ladder.

She sat on the top step and smiled at him. "What are you doing down there?"

"Thinking it would be really awesome if you wore a skirt the next time you put up crown molding."

She laughed. "Not going to happen."

"Then tell me this." He extended a hand to her, and she took it. "If I asked you to marry me, would *that* happen?"

"Are you asking me?"

He dropped to one knee when both of her feet hit the floor. "Now I am. Angela Corcarelli will you marry me? The ring will come later. Right now, I'm being impulsive and emotional."

"You're being passionate. I like when you're passionate."

"Like this?" He grabbed hold of her hands and tugged her to the floor beside him.

The kiss that followed melted her body and soul.

"Yes," she said as soon as their lips unlocked, and then she lifted his T-shirt over his head and smoothed her hands over his shoulders. "That answers both of your questions."

He kissed her again, flattening his palms against her ass and holding her lower body hard against his.

"We're going to be late to this party, aren't we?" she asked.

"Probably."

"I can handle that."

They had an awful lot to celebrate.

About the Author

Elley Arden is a born and bred Pennsylvanian who has lived as far west as Utah and as far north as Wisconsin. She drinks wine like it's water (a slight exaggeration), prefers a night at the ballpark to a night on the town, and believes almond English toffee is the key to happiness. Elley writes contemporary romances for Crimson Romance. For a complete list of Elley's books, visit *www.elleyarden.com*.

More from This Author

(From *Baby by Design* by Elley Arden)

"My God, he cleans up nice." Trish DeVign said the words around a mouthful of anise-flavored birthday cake while she stared at a suit-and-tie clad Tony Corcarelli. His colorful tattoos were covered by the sleeves of a fitted single-breasted jacket and navy dress shirt. His pitch-black hair was combed away from his face. And he'd shaved, leaving a slight contrast of color on his cheeks and chin, drawing her eyes straight to his unblemished lips.

"Too bad he's such a screw up."

Trish tore her gaze from Tony to level her best friend with the stink eye. "That's not a nice thing to say about your brother."

"It's true. Look at him playing paper football with the kids while he's dressed in an $800 suit. He should try spending less on clothes, keeping more of that money in the bank, and acting like a grown-up once in a while."

Trish sighed as the sinfully handsome man flicked a white triangle across the table to the tune of children's cackles. "I think it's cute."

"You would. Shoot. Aunt Helen's got a slice of cake big enough to prompt diabetic shock. Where's my mother?" Angie whipped her head in all directions and growled. "I'll be back."

Alone in the midst of familial chaos, Trish tapped her nails on the bottom of her plate and looked around the banquet room of Cestone's Italian Restaurant. Four generations of Corcarellis were a sight to be seen; a sight that made her smile even though it made her heart hurt. In the corner of the room, middle-aged women fussed over the food tables, directing servers, corralling cookies, and spearing meatballs, while in the center of the room, middle-aged men ate until their belt buckles popped. All around, the older generation talked…and talked…and talked, punctuating every sentence with nodding heads and waving hands. She loved them all, but it was the children that tethered her heart, tugging her toward their joyful noises.

"Tony, me next. I'll kick your as…"

Trish surmised the kid to be about twelve, and when he noticed her approaching, he bit off his last word amid oohs and ahhs from other kids around the table.

With sheepish eyes he looked from her to his cousin. "I'll beat you is all. That's what I was gonna say, Tony. Honestly."

"Sure you were," Tony said with a grin that tightened the tether on Trish's heart. "Just gimme ten minutes to throw some cake down my throat and I'm all yours." He stood, smoothed a hand down the button line of his suit coat, and blinded her with the full power of his male magnetism. All it took was a crooked smile, one that created a dark dip in his left cheek, not quite a dimple—no, dimples were too cute for a man this…edgy. "Hey, Boss Lady. I'd ask you to join me for cake, but I see you beat me to it."

Trish looked down at her empty plate and swallowed the ridiculous butterflies that escaped their netting whenever Tony came around. "What can I say? It was delicious."

He grinned again. "In that case, you should have another."

She'd been raised by a bone-skinny woman who espoused never eating a second serving of anything. Despite the doctrine being tattooed on Trish's brain, Tony Corcarelli was the kind of guy who could convince a girl to splurge. A classic bad boy, he was capable of more harm than good. But the good… *Mmm. Mmm. Mmm.*

Trish shook her head, scattering the thoughts that had her wallowing in adolescent purgatory, and reached for a more comfortable, competent topic. "How's the Jorgen's sofa coming along?"

"Should be done tomorrow. I can have the wingbacks ready next week." There wasn't a wrinkle on or around his lips, just smooth, perfectly puffed skin that circled a mouth decorated with teeth so white they were a sin on a man that dark.

"That's fine. I'm still waiting on the completion of a couple inlaid rugs, but the sooner the better. I want to keep this project on time." She sounded professional…and uptight, which was out of place for their surroundings but so much better than sounding like a crushing teen.

"So don't go changing the fabric on me again." He dropped his chin to his chest and regarded her through wide, smoky eyes. "Ya hear?" And then he winked.

Her stomach tumbled, churning the cake she'd eaten into cream.

"There you are." Jackson wrapped a sweaty hand around her bicep. "I have to go."

Tony lifted his full brows. "Duty calls, Doc?"

"Something like that."

But Trish knew better. Jackson wasn't on-call. He simply wasn't fond of the Corcarellis, something she'd learned on the car ride to the restaurant when he called them "Jersey Shore without the booze." The comment nagged Trish until she couldn't dismiss it as a poor attempt at humor, so she added it to the mental column of negatives vs. positives she kept for all her dates.

"Enjoy the rest of your evening, kids," Tony said with another crooked grin and a bob of his brows as he maneuvered around them. It was the kind of look that insinuated the rest of Trish's evening would be filled with hot, sticky, adventurous sex.

Trish would be lucky if she got a goodnight kiss. Looking up at prune-faced Jackson, she sighed. Three dates in, and already the negatives assigned to his list dipped perilously close to the kiss-off line.

"Tony, wait." A frilly-dressed, raven-haired girl shoved between Trish and Jackson to scurry after Tony.

Trish watched Tony turn and catch his little cousin as she leapt into his arms. The heartfelt, unscripted gesture made her smile, but when she turned back to Jackson he was scowling.

"These people have no manners," he grumbled. "And too many kids."

Thirty minutes later, after enough goodbyes, *arrivedercis*, and double-cheek kisses, Trish tucked inside Jackson's Porsche and listened to his continued complaints.

"That was a waste of three hours."

"I disagree. Nonna turning eighty-five is a big deal."

He rolled his eyes. "She's not *your* grandmother. None of those people are related to you—thank God. You could've sent a card and some flowers. Why subject yourself to that circus?"

That circus was all Trish wanted from life—not that specific circus, but a circus of her own. Loud, brash, unconditional love, not the kind of love that was earned by good behavior and hefty bankrolls. She sighed, because this part of getting to know someone in order to ascertain compatibility was always the most uncomfortable. "I'm adopted."

"Oh." He glanced at her as he adjusted his grip on the steering wheel. "I didn't know that."

Considering how much Jackson adored her surgeon father and socialite mother, she couldn't help but wonder if he was disappointed she didn't share the sacred DeVign genes.

"It's not really a big deal until I'm around a family like the Corcarellis," Trish continued. "Then I start to wonder what my biological family is like."

Road noise swirled between them as she waited patiently for his reaction.

He snorted. "If you ask me, that's dangerous thinking. I mean obviously you're better off now. Look how lucky you are. Hell, I'd stand in line to be adopted by the DeVigns."

She bet he would. "Yes, well, there's something to be said for knowing where you came from. Don't you think?"

"If I came from a family like the Corcarellis, I'd never want to know. Somebody needs to gift them with a lifetime supply of birth control so they stop polluting the gene pool." He laughed.

She clenched her hands in her lap and stared out the window at the shadowy shapes and lighted signs flying by. "I'll skip the nightcap, Jackson. Just drop me off at home."

"Oh. Hey." He slowed at a stoplight and stretched an arm across the top of her headrest. "I was kidding. I mean, they're accommodating enough. They're just rough around the edges, and it takes some getting used to." He smiled as he leaned closer, and for a second, hope bubbled in Trish's chest. "For a guy like me who'd rather have non-anesthetized surgery than kids, it's a real stretch to relate."

Every one of those stupid, hope-filled bubbles popped. "The light is green," she said, redirecting his attention to the road and her attention to the nauseous pit in her stomach.

She was tired of this; tired of getting her hopes up only to have them trashed. At thirty-two, according to her calculations, eight good baby-making years remained. She'd spent the last two years methodically dating, hoping for a ring and white dress. But when she imagined a lifetime with each prospect, and concluded it was more like a life sentence, she lowered her standards. After all, she was an independent woman who didn't need a man to help her raise a child. But she did need a man to help her make one…and for more than his sperm. She wanted his family history, too. The impersonal, anonymity of creating a baby with a bodiless stranger from a donor clinic wouldn't work. She wanted her baby to have a complete medical history, intergenerational stories, and at least a quarterly look at his or her dad.

"Are you sure you don't want that nightcap?" He parked in front of her house and flashed a suggestive grin.

"I'm sure." She'd rather have a baby. "My stomach isn't feeling right."

"Maybe it was the cake," he said as she opened the car door. "Who likes anise birthday cake anyway?"

She stood up and spun around. "I like anise birthday cake." And with that, she slammed the car door on his bewildered face.

"I'll call you tomorrow," he sputtered out his open window as she clip-clopped around the front of the car to her stone walk.

Don't bother, she thought.

Talk about a disappointing night. She should've had a second piece of cake.

• • •

Tony pulled the burlap tight around the wingchair's retied springs and fired staples from his gun into the wooden frame. He could tell a lot about a person by the condition of their furniture. This particular piece belonged to a newly minted chief of radiology and his wife, a friend of Trish. Before Tony could repair the split and crumbling frame, he'd had to remove three layers of dollar-table, outdated fabric, foul-smelling Dacron, and way too much foam rubber. The haphazard upholsteries told a rags-to-riches tale. When Tony was done, these once sad and neglected chairs would flank the finest fireplace in a Trish DeVign-decorated home. Something that didn't come cheap.

"Why don't you ever answer your freaking phone? Ma's been trying to get ahold of us all day." Angie barged into the garage like she owned the place… Well, technically she did. It was attached to her house, but Tony paid rent to use the space as his sometimes-upholstery shop. He couldn't very well upholster sofa-sized items in his downtown efficiency.

He kept his eyes on the staple line. "What's wrong with your phone?"

"My phone? I was onsite all day. You expect me to hear a phone ringing over a floor sander? You weren't here, were you? You were out on your bike."

"Maybe. What's it matter to you?"

"It matters, Tony. It matters."

That's what the women in his life—and there were a lot of them—were always telling him. Nonna, Ma, Angie, and his aunts were forever pressing him to sell the bike, cover the tattoos, and quit playing with furniture so he could take his place at the helm of Pop's carpentry company.

No, thank you.

Becoming a carpenter and taking over the business hadn't done Angie any good. The responsibility robbed her of free time and fun. Besides, Tony already owned his own business, contracting out his upholstery services. The business was small and nondescript, which left his freedom intact.

"What'd Ma want?" he asked, rather than stoke his sister's perennially pissy mood by defending his life's direction.

"I don't know. I can't reach her now. The line's busy. How hard is it to get call waiting and caller ID?"

For a woman who still couldn't figure out the TV remote? Hard.

Strains of "Born to Be Wild" echoed above the air compressor.

"That's her," Angie yelled, pointing in the direction of his phone.

"You answer it," Tony said, preferring to spare himself the gory details of which cousin said what, more than a week ago at Nonna's birthday party, and why aunts X, Y, and Z were no longer speaking.

Angie kicked his thigh with her steel-toed boot as she walked by on her way to answer his phone. "Why is nothing ever important to you?"

As he listened to his sister answer their mother's call, he winced at his stinging thigh and traded the staple gun for an old-fashioned hammer and tacks. Wailing on the metal wedges would help. He had news for his too-serious-for-her-own-good sister, lots of things were important to him. Fun topped the list, with happiness running a close second, followed by friends who fed the fun and happiness.

"Oh God, no," Angie sobbed, and then wailed. "Tony, Nonna has ovarian cancer."

The mallet slipped from his hand.

As much as they drove him crazy, family was important, too.

An hour later, Tony was packed like a sardine into Nonna's galley kitchen with a collection of aunts and uncles who watched the stricken woman stir sauce despite the horrible news.

"I give it to God," she announced, raising one palm to the ceiling. "I no take it back."

There were a few amens, but as Tony looked around the room, he was struck by the paleness of the usually olive faces. And there were tears, but only when Nonna wasn't looking. And there were whispers of sentences he couldn't quite catch.

Stage IV. Too late for surgery. Chemo. Radiation. Prayers.

He felt sick, like he swallowed a jar of lug nuts and couldn't cough them up, let alone crap them out. And when the bowls of food started around the table, he couldn't eat.

He pushed away his chair, knowing the bathroom was the only rational escape. If he left the house, someone was bound to snitch, and once again he'd be a disappointment; the Corcarelli son not man enough to face the truth. Away from the heavy emotions, he flipped the lid down on the toilet and pulled his cell phone from his pocket. Rather than dwell on the turmoil twisting his guts in knots, he'd dwell on his fantasy football team's lousy performance. His wide receivers tanked, and there were never any good ones available after the draft.

Tap. Tap. Tap.

Tony looked at the door. "Occupied." And yet he couldn't stay much longer, knowing someone waited, unless he wanted to look like an inconsiderate pig. So he hurried up and dropped a running back, picked up a defense, and took a deep breath before he opened the bathroom door.

Nonna stood on the other side. "Antonio." She smooshed his cheeks in her scratchy, onion-scented hands and smiled the saddest smile he'd ever seen.

All he could do was hug her, squish her weathered body against him and wish he were strong enough to expunge the cancer with one good squeeze. "Love you, Nonna."

She pushed out of the hug and patted his cheek. "Why you want to be alone?"

Of all things…she was bringing up his marital status today. "I'm not alone, Nonna. I have all of you."

Both of her hands patted his face. "Life should be shared."

"And I *am* sharing my life." He slid his hands around her wrists and held them in his.

"No wife. No *bebe*." She nodded. "You make a good priest."

He bit back a laugh. A tattooed, Harley-riding priest. Come to think of it, he'd like to see that. But not him. No way. He was pretty sure celibacy was bad for his health.

"I'm fine, Nonna."

But she wasn't.

She nodded and shuffled past him to the bathroom. He wondered if she was going in to get away—like him. But if losing Pops taught him anything, it was that cancer left nowhere to hide.

"Tony, you need to be out here for this." Ma poked her head into the hallway and flagged him back into the dining room.

Aunt Josie was speed talking in a whisper when he walked into the room. "How do you know she can fly?"

"I'll check with the doctor," Aunt Carmella said.

"I think it's a wonderful idea," Ma added.

"Aunt Carmella and Uncle Gene have offered to take Nonna back to Lucca for a couple weeks," Angie explained in Tony's ear. "And when she gets back from Italy, Aunt Jo and Uncle Mike are going to surprise her by flying her brother in from California. Sort of like a surprise bucket list."

Tony nodded. A lot could happen during ten minutes holed up in a bathroom.

"I'm going to become Catholic," Ma announced. Her sisters-in-law gasped.

Angie flashed a look at Tony. Even Dad's illness hadn't prompted a gesture like that. But in the years after his death, Ma and Nonna had grown close, close enough that Ma declared her the mother she'd never had. And now this? Talk about grand gestures.

Tony watched as Angie wrapped her arms around their mother's neck and squeezed. "I want to do something, too," Angie said. "I'll have to think about it though. Tony, what about you?"

If the burn from the air hitting his wide eyes was any indication, he looked like a deer in headlights. His family stared back at him.

"Take your time, Tony. Something will come to you."

But all around him, they didn't look convinced.

Nonna shuffled into the kitchen. "*Mangia. Mangia.*" She pointed at the table full of food.

With the conversation stalled, everyone took their seats and ate—everyone except for Tony. He stared at his pasta, in between glances at Nonna. His family was united in giving her months—hopefully years—to remember. They expected him to join in. He'd ignored their expectations without a care before, but this time was different.

Something will come to you.

Nonna slurped a noodle into her mouth and offered him a small smile. She wanted him to join the priesthood or fall in love.

Anyway Tony looked at it, he was screwed.

For more books by Elley Arden, check out:

The Kemmons Brothers Baseball Series

Save My Soul

Change My Mind

Heal My Heart

Take Me Out

Harmony Falls Novels

Crashing the Congressman's Wedding

Battling the Best Man

Marrying the Wrong Man

Praise for the Harmony Falls series:

"The ending was my all-time favorite . . . This is definitely an AMAZING book that I recommend to all!"—Mamival's Books

"Good things come when you least expect it—at least I did with this book. I didn't expect to laugh, cry, and fall in love. But Elley Arden did those things to me, and after that short read, I think I'm coming back for more from this author."—Book Freak

Emerald Springs Legacy

Trouble Brewing

Chad's Chance

In the mood for more Crimson Romance?
Check out *Text Me* by Shelley K. Wall at *CrimsonRomance.com*.